HOW TO CREATE A MONSTER

John Ward

Scareville
Series by: John Ward

Published by Crystal Lake Publishing
Where Stories Come Alive!

www.crystallakepub.com

First publication by John Ward in 2023
Current version copyright 2025 John Ward
Join the Crystal Lake community today
on our newsletter and Patreon!
https://linktr.ee/CrystalLakePublishing

For our mature horror books
download our latest catalog here:
https://geni.us/CLPCatalog

ISBN: 978-1-964398-72-3

Cover art:
Jorge Iracheta

Follow us on Amazon:

WELCOME
TO ANOTHER

CRYSTAL LAKE PUBLISHING
CREATION

Join today at www.crystallakepub.com & www.patreon.com/CLP

I WANT YOU FOR
SCAREVILLE
EST 20 25
ARMY
JOIN NOW!

Prologue

What you are about to experience will send shivers down your spine. A book series that will leave you questioning everything you thought you knew about things that go bump in the night.

Are you brave enough to come along on a journey that is sure to induce fear, nightmares, and leave you questioning if it's worth leaving your bed for that midnight snack? Very well! Please be sure to buckle up and always keep your arms and legs inside the ride as we delve into....

How To Create a Monster

1.

Halloween has always been a huge deal in my hometown of Buford, Georgia. Most places have a few houses that participate in decorating and trick or treating, but Buford *really* gets into Halloween.

Starting in the last week of September, everything in town is consumed by Halloween. Geno's Halloween Store's grand opening begins the festivities every year. There's a contest for the largest pumpkin in town, as well as a car-crushing celebration where the winner gets to witness their prized gourd raised high in the air by a crane and then sent free-falling down onto the old clunker beneath it. It never seems to end, and our whole town gets into it. We also hold a giant parade which is always a spectacle.

Everyone in town goes all out decorating their yards and homes. Buford has a voting committee which votes for the best-decorated yard every year. My family and the Blankenship family have been in the midst of a Halloween decorating war ever since I was a little girl. The Blankenships live across the street and have won the last two years in a row. My dad vowed to bring the title back home this year.

Over the last few years, however, it seemed like things had changed. Everyone was so focused on dressing up in cute or silly costumes that fewer families were decorating for Halloween. Most of those who did partake, were going the cute and silly route as well.

The change happened like the flip of a light switch a few years ago. I'm thirteen years old now, but when I was younger, Halloween was a scary time.

Thinking about it makes me upset. My parents raised me with the understanding that Halloween was a spooky time of the year. All in good fun of course.

"You ready to go?" my dad asked impatiently, as he motioned toward the door.

"I'm coming," Mom replied frantically, struggling with her second shoe.

Today was *the* big day. The grand opening of Geno's Halloween Store. The whole town was sure to be in a tizzy. My dad and I stared intently at Mom. Dad tapped vigorously on his wristwatch. When she finished and came walking by, she stuck her tongue out at him. We darted out to the driveway and hopped into the SUV. All of us prepared to snag the best decorations we could find.

"This is it, honey. This is the year we take back the crown," my dad said as we sped out of the driveway.

"Whatever you say dear," Mom replied with a chuckle as Dad cranked up Halloween music for the drive.

My mom and dad make the perfect team. My dad is a visionary, while my mom is the artistic one who makes things come true.

Everyone tells me I am the perfect combination of my parents. According to my family, I look a lot like my mom. I have her brunette shoulder-length hair and slim figure. My dad is of stocky build, bald and has a big burly beard. Apparently, I got his sense of humor.

My dad is a contractor and owns his own construction business, while my mom works at the local art museum and sells her drawings and paintings on the side. Interestingly enough, I'm artistic just like my mom but share the same vision and determination as my dad.

Our favorite Halloween song from Dad's playlist began, and my dad yelled. "Here we go!" as he slapped the steering wheel. I couldn't help but grin as I stared out my window, watching our neighborhood as we drove by. It's a modest town. Almost all the homes are very close together and were built in the early 1900s. They all have that rustic charm.

I remembered then, how every single home in our neighborhood used to deck out their yards with the creepiest Halloween decorations. Those were fun times. Anymore, it seems as though Halloween has become more cartoony. Luckily, there were still a few families--including mine--that went all out, making sure Halloween remained scary.

"Oh, my goodness," Mom muttered as we pulled up to a stoplight at Broad Street. We could see Geno's Halloween store, and the parking lot was already packed.

Geno's had moved to the opposite end of town a few years ago. Business was so good he'd doubled the size of his store to keep up with the demand.

The store was now located in a former department store that had closed. It was *absolutely massive.*

"Well, we're just going to have to make the most of it," Dad said glumly. "You have the list, right honey?"

My mom dug around in her purse for a moment, "Yep! Got it right here!"

"Perfect," Dad said as he parked the car. "Let's get ready to *RUUUMBLE!*" He sounded as though he was going to announce the main event of a boxing match.

2.

It looked as though the entire town was already crammed into Geno's. It was an absolute madhouse inside the store. A flurry of kids ran around, playing with all the animatronics, while their parents glanced around the store trying to find the perfect decorations for their yards.

I knew my two best friends were probably in the store, so I tugged on my dad's hoodie.

"Yes, Emily?" he asked softly, as he skimmed over his list.

"Would it be alright if I go find Ben and Liz? I am sure they're here too," I replied.

"That's fine." My dad glanced down at his watch. "It's 11:07 right now, just be sure to meet me and Mom at the car at noon."

"Thanks, Dad!" I replied. My dad had given me my very own watch for my thirteenth birthday. I was glad I'd decided to wear it today, as I wasn't allowed to have a cell phone yet.

"Sure thing, jellybean," he replied, as he and Mom headed off toward the static props and animatronics to look around.

He was the king of Dad Jokes. I found them humorous. Normally Mom rolled her eyes at them.

I made my way through the store. The place was so big, finding Liz and Ben would be like trying to find a needle in a haystack. Between all the people, the loud animatronics, and the Halloween music blaring, Geno's was a sensory overload. I loved every second of it.

I walked through aisle after aisle of decorations before making my way to the giant section of costumes. The area went on forever and had everything from baby costumes to silly costumes, to the most terrifying costumes you could think of. They also had a long row of high-end masks hanging on the wall, stretching across the entire back of the store.

I felt bummed out that I hadn't found Ben or Liz yet. I thought for sure they'd be here.

"Booga! Booga! Booga!" yelled several figures in masks, as I turned the corner into another row of costumes. It caught me off guard, and I couldn't help but let out a shriek.

My scream was met with laughter as the four people lifted their masks. My arch enemies, Sierra and Kelly, as well as their boyfriends, Bryce and Tyler, stood in the aisle.

Sierra and Kelly were both prissy, blonde princesses. Their boyfriends were hulking jocks. Bryce had blonde hair as well, but Tyler had dark brown hair.

"Oh, we got you so good!" Sierra mocked as they burst out in laughter.

Sierra was the daughter of my neighbors across the street, the Blankenships. She and I had been best friends from the moment we first learned to crawl. Unfortunately, over the years, we had drifted apart. She had become a snooty princess, and now we hated each other's guts. I rolled my eyes at her.

"Yeah, good one," I replied, trying to make my way around them.

The four of them blocked my path as Sierra responded with, "I don't even know why you're in the costume section, you're already scary looking as it is!"

Several other kids nearby heard her joke, and boisterous laughter filled the air. My blood boiled. I hated bullies.

"Just leave me alone," I cried. I tried to turn back the way I'd come but tripped when Kelly stuck her foot out in front of me.

I landed with a hard *thud* on the floor and everyone around me laughed again. My eyes welled up with tears.

"Just thought I'd save you the trip," taunted Kelly as she high-fived Sierra.

"Don't worry Emily, we're going to win the best yard contest again this year. You guys should just donate your second-hand decorations," Sierra mocked.

"Leave her alone," I heard a familiar voice call out from a distance.

I turned to look and, sure enough, it was Ben! Not far behind him was Liz.

"What are you going to do about it, String Bean?" Bryce spat at Ben.

Ben ignored him as he helped me off the floor. Liz brushed my clothes off.

"Go talk to someone who cares," Liz said, and gave them a shoo motion with her hand.

"Whatever, let's get out of here guys," Sierra replied. They marched away, still cackling amongst themselves.

"Are you alright?" Ben asked.

"I'm better now. I just hate those guys. They're a bunch of jerks," I responded.

"Well, they won't be bothering you anymore," Liz replied.

I was so thankful for my two best friends. I'd been friends with both since first grade, but I'd developed a crush on Ben over the last couple of years.

Ben was such a sweetheart. He wasn't your typical jock, or even an outcast for that matter. He got along with pretty much everyone. He was a social butterfly, always dressed in sporty clothes, and loved football. He had curly light brown hair and a slim build.

Liz was very similar to me, with the exception that her hair was all black. Like me, she was also very artistic and spent a lot of her time reading books.

"Want to go look at the animatronics?" Ben offered while we waited for the crowd that had formed around me to thin out.

"That is the most romantic thing anyone has ever said to me," I joked. The three of us chuckled.

"I thought you'd never ask," Liz added with another laugh. "Let's go!"

We had made our way to the large animatronics on display. Everything looked so cool. There were little pads you stepped on which activated them and made them move around and talk or make frightening noises.

My favorite was a hunched over werewolf. When you activated it, it growled and then slowly stood upright, howling as its mouth opened wide. Its eyes glowed red. It was ginormous! Had to be at least 12 feet tall when it was fully upright.

I was having a blast with Ben and Liz. This was easily my favorite time of year.

Just as we were about to make our way to the last couple of animatronics, I heard a loud crash near the front of the store and heard my dad yelling afterward.

I looked over. Dad and Mom had a cart filled with decorations and a big flat dolly covered with boxes. Apparently, a couple of boxes had toppled off the dolly and my dad was scrambling to pick them up.

I couldn't help but laugh. It looked like something straight out of a cartoon.

I glanced down at my watch and noticed it was almost noon. I turned to Ben and Liz. I told them I had to go but would see them tonight and we could walk around the neighborhood to look at all the decorations.

I walked outside to meet my parents at the car. From a distance, I could see that my dad was scratching his head and looking back and forth from the car to the boxes. Clearly, he was trying to figure out how to make it all fit.

"Are you sure we can get all of this in one trip?" my mom asked as I walked up.

My dad looked at the car, and then back at the boxes, and then back at the car again. He frowned and then shrugged. "Yeah, I don't think it will be an issue. We have the third row we can fold down. From there, it's just simple geometry."

"Okay, if you say so, honey," she replied. She smirked and shook her head while we sat in the car and Dad tried to figure out how to fit everything in.

Unfortunately for me and Mom, the simple geometry turned into our having boxes piled on our laps, while the entire car was packed to the brim with decorations.

As we pulled into our driveway, my dad had the audacity to ask, "See, that wasn't so bad now, was it?"

We groaned as he got out of the car.

"Huh, looks like the Blankenships are getting home now too. Hey Ken!" Dad said as he waved at them.

"Ronnie, if you don't get us out of this car this instant..." my mom said angrily. Dad hurried around the car and pulled out the boxes that were smooshing us.

When we finally got out of the car, Mom and Dad joked around with one another as they unloaded the boxes and placed them in the driveway.

I glanced over at the Blankenships' house. They were doing the same. Their house was very similar to ours. Both were three story homes. Both had white vinyl siding. The only difference was that theirs had blue shutters and a red front door. Ours had black shutters and a black front door.

Sierra shot me an evil grin from across the road. I had to look away. Her mere presence was enough to irritate me. I couldn't believe she and her friends had bullied me on opening day at Geno's.

"Why don't you go over there and say hi to Sierra?" my dad asked, as he set another heavy box down in the driveway.

My parents knew we didn't hang out anymore but were completely oblivious to the fact that Sierra had turned into a bully.

"No thanks," I replied, as I grabbed one of the final boxes. "I want to help decorate."

"Heck yeah! Up high!" he exclaimed, reaching out for a high five.

I shook my head and grinned but gave him the high five he waited for.

Mom interrupted our moment. "Emily, go get the inventory list on the kitchen counter. Then, go into the basement and start bringing up some of our old decorations while your dad and I unbox all the new ones."

"But I wanna see what we got today!" I groaned.

"Don't worry, we won't start without you," Mom said, patting me on the shoulder.

"Fine." I quickly made my way inside.

When I entered the kitchen, I heard clanking above me. Startled, I looked up and saw a grey flash flying right at me.

I let out a frightened yelp, before realizing it was our cat Smoky.

I always theorized that Smoky enjoyed Halloween and horror too. He was constantly hiding and jumping out at us at the most random times, trying to scare us. He was a Russian blue cat that we had adopted several years ago, and he fit into our family so well. His silvery–grey fur was what gave him his name.

"Dang it Smoky!" I snapped as he scurried across the kitchen and out of sight.

He is always up to no good, I thought with a grin as I picked up the inventory list.

I didn't *really* need the list. There were tubs in the basement clearly marked **Halloween.**

Nonetheless, I folded the paper and stuffed it into my jeans pocket. I then headed downstairs and slowly dragged the tubs up one by one.

We had accumulated many Halloween decorations over the years. Some families would be appalled by the number of decorations we had. Everything from skeletons to headstones, to zombie creatures, as well as a bunch of different colored lights.

I could hardly contain my excitement as I dragged the last tub out onto the front porch.

Mom and Dad were already busy working away on the graveyard scene in our front yard. They had planted several headstones into the ground. Mom worked on placing the zombie props around the graves, while Dad ran wires out to the yard to add lighting.

"What can I do to help?" I asked.

"Help your mother stage the cemetery," my dad grunted, as he bent over to plug in the lights he'd set around the yard.

We were working like a well-oiled machine on this beautiful early fall day, and soon, everything was set up and in the right place. We had assembled our graveyard and equipped it with what appeared to be zombies coming up out of the graves. We also added a bunch of green moss to the headstones, zombies, and surrounding grass to give it a creepy swamp vibe.

On our porch, we set up a table with all our skeletons sitting around it, playing a card game. My dad had also bought and installed a couple of creepy clown animatronics in the yard. They were motion-activated and would say creepy phrases and then bellow out their creepy clown laughs. While he had done that, Mom and I had done all the staging of the props and yard effects.

Dusk drew nearer as my dad eagerly turned on the power strip which connected the extension cords to everything.

Immediately, our house was painted in an array of green lighting from the cemetery scene while orange light flooded the porch over the skeletons and other props. The only thing missing were our jack-o-lanterns. We would need to wait another couple of weeks so they wouldn't rot before Halloween.

"It's beautiful," Dad said as he sprinted around the front of the house and joined us.

We were enjoying the fruits of our labor when Mr. Blankenship called from across the road, "Hey Ronnie!" Apparently, they had just finished as well.

We all turned to the right just as everything in the Blankenships' yard lit up. It truly was a sight to behold. They had built an entire zombie circus set in their front yard. It had everything from the big red and white striped tent to zombies and creepy clowns staged in the front yard. They looked as though they were battling one another.

Light from red and white floodlights cascaded over the yard. The most demoralizing part came when I noticed they'd purchased the giant werewolf animatronic I loved. They'd even gone so far as to dress it in a clown outfit.

Their whole yard looked amazing.

We had been so busy working on our decorations that none of us had taken the time to notice their display until just now. We were left speechless as we slowly made our way inside.

Dad seemed to be pretty bummed out as he and Mom sat on the couch sipping apple cider from their mugs. I could tell they thought the Blankenships' yard was better than ours once again. The Blankenships did something different every year and somehow always managed to outdo their previous year's decorating.

"Do you wanna walk around the neighborhood and look at everyone else's decorations?" I asked my parents, as I plopped on the recliner next to the couch. I tried to sound upbeat as I sipped on my apple cider as well.

My dad glanced up. He looked defeated. "Not tonight sweetie," he replied as he sank back into the couch.

"Well then, would it be alright if I have Ben and Liz come over so we can walk around the neighborhood and look around?" I asked.

"That's fine, Emily," my mom said. "Just don't be out too late."

In a lot of cities, it's probably unsafe for kids to wander around their neighborhood without their parents, but on grand opening night for Geno's Halloween store, it had become a rite of passage. Police were always out in force, patrolling everywhere, while kids and parents alike scampered around the neighborhood looking at everyone else's decorations.

This was the first time my mom and dad didn't seem interested in going. It bummed me out, but I was looking forward to hanging out with Ben and Liz.

I chugged the rest of my apple cider and hopped up from the couch. I headed into the kitchen to call Ben and Liz.

My friends lived a couple of streets over, each on opposite sides of my house. It wouldn't be long before they arrived. I waved to my parents as I headed out the front door.

Night had finally fallen over Buford, Georgia. Excitement flowed through my veins as I hopped down the steps and waited for Ben and Liz to arrive.

I couldn't help but stare at the Blankenships across the street. A huge crowd of people had already formed around their house, posing with and taking photos of their yard, while our decorations went largely unnoticed.

I could see why my dad was so upset. We had worked so hard, and our yard looked the best it had ever looked. It just wasn't enough to garner the admiration of the community.

"Hey, Emily!" I heard Liz shout, snapping me out of the trance-like state I'd been in. She ran up and gave me a big hug.

I appreciated the hug, needing that positivity. "Hey, girl," I replied.

"Your yard looks so good! We didn't even decorate this year," Liz exclaimed as she stepped back and admired all the hard work that we had put in.

Moments later, Ben came running up the driveway as well.

"Yooo! Did you guys see the Blankenship house?" He beamed at us and Liz and I both shot him an angry glance. "Oh, b-but you guys did really great too, Emily!"

"Thanks," I replied, trying to convince myself it was equally good. "I know it's not as flashy as the Blankenships' house, but I still think it looks really creepy!"

"It does for sure!" both Liz and Ben answered simultaneously, trying too hard to show their support.

"Aw, thanks guys," I replied with a chuckle, as we marched out to the sidewalk and began perusing the neighborhood.

There were a couple of neat houses nearby. One had purple and orange lights illuminating their yard and home. They had it decorated with witch-themed decorations and props.

The family in another cool house must've gotten busy ahead of time with carving jack-o-lanterns, as they had dozens of them all over the yard. They also had some creepy scarecrow props staged in the front.

All the other decorations seemed too silly and childish. Most of the yards we passed had cartoon characters dressed in Halloween costumes. Some yards had badly done cobwebs around their bushes. Others had old ghost decorations hanging from their tree branches.

"I miss when our whole neighborhood used to take Halloween more seriously," I said as we passed another home with cartoony inflatables in their front yard.

"Yeah, Halloween season used to be a lot spookier," Ben replied as we made our way toward his house.

When we made it to Ben's yard, I couldn't believe my eyes. It was decorated with an inflatable T-rex dressed like a pirate. They also had a cartoony inflatable ghost, as well as some inflatable jack-o-lanterns.

"Ben?" I cried out in disbelief. "What...is this?"

"Look, I can't help I have a 6-year-old sister," he replied, staring down at the sidewalk.

"No, no, no! Don't go blaming Gabby!" Liz fired back with a laugh. "I heard you tell your parents you thought the T-rex was cool!"

I let out a fake gasp as I jokingly glared at Ben.

"T-Rexes *are* cool!" Ben cried.

"Well, I guess this is what Halloween has become. It's no longer about being scary. It's just silly decorations and silly costumes. No one takes it seriously anymore," I said.

"It is kinda crazy to think about...like...what happened?" Liz responded, sounding confused herself.

"You know, in ancient times, Halloween was the time when the veil between the living and the dead was at its thinnest. What's scarier than that?" I asked.

Neither Ben nor Liz could come up with an answer, so I just kept rambling as we leaned against the fence in Ben's front yard.

"I mean, just based on history and tradition it should stay scary. Why can't it go back to the way things used to be?"

"Yeah, maybe one day," Ben replied with a hint of doubt. He headed back toward his house. "I'll catch up with you guys later."

5.

Liz returned to her house as I made my way back home. As I neared the house, I saw Sierra standing at the end of our driveway, grinning from ear to ear.

I rolled my eyes and sighed.

"What do you want, Sierra?" I asked, filled with dread.

"That's no way to greet your neighbor," she sneered. "I just wanted to compliment you on your yard."

"Thanks," I moved around her and headed toward the front door.

"They say a blind squirrel finds a nut every once in a while. Maybe you guys will win the contest in the next decade," she joked.

I ignored her and slammed our front door shut. My parents were on the couch watching an old black-and-white horror film. I stormed up the steps and into my bedroom.

My bedroom wasn't anything special. I had posters of actors and boy bands, mostly guys I had crushes on. I also had a lot of Halloween stuff taped to my walls, and a desk I used to practice drawing. Other than that, it was a normal room for someone my age. It had a bed, nightstand, and a dresser.

I was filled with a mix of emotions. It had been a long day.

I think the thing that bothered me the most right now, was the fact that Halloween itself just didn't feel the same anymore. Aside from my family, the Blankenships, and a few others, it seemed like Buford treated Halloween as just another silly holiday. I hated it.

It felt like the Halloween spirit was gone. I wish I could change that. I turned on my lamp, headed over to my desk, and pulled out a sketch pad and a pencil. Then, I began to daydream about what I thought the Spirit of Halloween might look like and started drawing on my sketchpad.

I wish Halloween was scary again.

The pencil seemed to naturally flow to the vision I had conjured up in my brain. I drew more and more, getting as detailed as my brain would allow, channeling my mom's abilities.

As I completed the drawing, I couldn't help but stare at it in amazement. It was the best artwork I had ever done!

I had drawn my rendition of the Spirit of Halloween, and it was both frightening and glorious. Though it had a giant pumpkin head, it wasn't your typical jack-o-lantern, no. I made him red and white swirl lollipop eyes, a green gumdrop nose, and a carved smile. I drew candy corn teeth within that creepy, demented smile. His head was topped off with a long, spirally green stem.

It had a broad body, and I colored it in a black-and-white plaid shirt, dark blue jeans, boots and green hands with long green leafy fingers. The things that made me most proud were the details I'd captured in the face and hands. It was truly unique and terrifying.

I stood up and admired my work before changing into my pajamas. Then, I laid on my bed and looked at the drawing one more time.

"I wish you were real," I said aloud. "And I wish you would make Halloween scary again."

I turned my lamp off to try to sleep, but I struggled for a while to get comfy. The wind outside howled angrily. It was absolutely tearing through the trees outside. Strange, considering how beautiful the weather had been all day long.

My eyes grew heavy, and I found myself thinking more and more about my drawing. *MY* Spirit of Halloween. I found myself wishing and praying that it would come to life and bring Halloween back to its once creepy pedestal again.

I began to imagine how he would come to life at night and would creep up on unsuspecting kids jumping out and screaming at them, leaving them terrified as they ran away.

He needs to vomit pumpkin guts too, yeah that's a nice touch. Gosh, it would be so cool if he were real.

Finally, I drifted off to sleep, completely content as I thought about all things Halloween.

Sometime in the middle of the night, I was startled awake by the sound of something tapping against my bedroom window. My heart was racing. Could it be?

My bedroom was slightly illuminated by the ambient lighting from our Halloween decorations out front. I slowly crept over to my bedroom window and looked outside.

The wind was still whipping extremely hard, causing a tree branch to occasionally tap on my window. Part of me was relieved I hadn't seen some sort of horrendous monster staring up at me, but part of me was also disappointed.

I turned back toward my bed, and suddenly, my cat Smoky let out a horrifying shriek as he leaped off the floating shelf I had above my bed. He bounced off my head as he darted off to somewhere else in my room.

"Jeez, Smoky!" I gasped. "What has gotten into you?"

It took a while for my heart rate to slow so that I could fall asleep. Smoky was on a tear today. Normally he'd pull these shenanigans maybe once a week, but never twice on the same day. He never scared me in my bedroom either. Weird.

The next morning, a knock at my bedroom door woke me from my slumber. Groggily, I stirred awake as my dad came into my room.

"Are you feeling okay, Emily?" my dad asked as he sat at the foot of my bed.

"Yeah, why?" I yawned as I glanced over at my alarm clock. It was almost noon. "Holy crap!"

"Yeah, you must've been tired," Dad replied with a chuckle as he hopped up from my bed. "We have to get a move on if we want decent seats today."

That's right! I'd almost forgotten. The day after Geno's Grand Opening, our town always does a big event called Pumpkin Fest. People from all over the area bring their largest pumpkins, and the heaviest one gets a cash prize. The main event of the evening is when they use a crane to drop the winning pumpkin onto a car. It was always mesmerizing to witness the gargantuan orange blob exploding into a million pieces with seeds and pumpkin guts flying everywhere and flattening the poor car into a pancake.

They also held pumpkin carving contests and other little activities. There were food trucks there as well. Every week-end between now and Halloween, there was always *something* Halloween related going on in Buford.

"I'm sorry, Dad. I'm up. I'll get dressed and we can go," I replied.

"It's okay honey. I just wanted to make sure you were feeling alright," he replied, brushing my hair with his hand.

He started to walk out of my room but stopped for a second and walked over to my desk.

"What's this?" he asked, picking up my drawing, his eyes growing wide.

"Oh, that? It...It's nothing," his lip curled as he looked at it and I wondered if he liked it.

"Nothing?" he asked, almost sounding offended. "Honey, this is amazing!"

"Really?"

"Yes!" He exclaimed as he examined the drawing further. "I have to show this to your mother. She will be so proud!"

And with that, he hurried out of my room.

They were discussing my drawing when I entered the kitchen. When they saw me, their eyes lit up.

"Emily, this drawing is so good!" my mom said.

"Thanks, Mom!" I wasn't sure how to react. I'd never had a response like this before.

Mom beamed. "Your father and I've decided we're going to turn your drawing into a Halloween decoration! We're going to the local hobby shop and get the materials to make it.".

"What? Really?"

"Yep! I think it will bring *just* the right amount of originality to our yard and help us win the contest too!" my dad replied. "*This* can't be bought at the store like everything else in this town. This is a Riggs custom piece!"

"Wow! This is so awesome! I don't know what to say! How are you going to make it?"

"We'll figure that out," he replied deep in thought. "We'll need to frame out a body and use latex and spray on foam. Then we'll have to carve and detail it from there."

"That's really cool. I can't wait to see how it turns out!"

"We can't either," my mom chimed in.

"Alright, enough chit-chatting. Let's head over to Gantzler Farm and grab some seats!" my dad said.

My drawing had brought the sparkle back into his eyes. I could tell they were filled with hope again. I'd had no idea, when I'd drawn my Spirit of Halloween last night, that it would have this sort of effect on my parents. But I was happy to see it.

7.

Pumpkin Fest is held every year on the outskirts of town at Gantzler Farm. They have a big corral where they hold rodeos and other events throughout the year, as well as a couple of barns and a ton of acreage they use to hold the festival.

We pulled up to the farm and found the parking lot already full. Cars had begun parking on the grass.

"Looks busy already. Hopefully, we can get good seats," Dad said, as he crammed our SUV in next to a little sedan.

As we headed up toward the entrance of Pumpkin Fest, I saw Ben and Liz standing off to the side of the entrance, waiting for me.

"Ben! Liz!" I yelled. I ran up and gave them both hugs. "Where are your parents?"

"They already went inside. Why are you always late? We've been waiting here for like twenty minutes," Ben said with a chuckle.

"Yeah, sorry. I totally overslept! I completely forgot about Pumpkin Fest today," I replied as my parents joined us.

"Hey Ben, hey Liz! How are you guys?" my dad asked as he and Mom walked up with friendly smiles.

"We're good, Mr. Riggs," both replied.

"I'm glad to hear it."

"Would it be okay with you guys if we hung out with Emily?" Ben asked.

My parents exchanged glances before my mom answered. "Oh sure, we'll go find your parents and try to sit next to them."

"Awesome! Thanks, Mr. and Mrs. Riggs!" Ben cried. We turned and walked through the entrance together.

"Emily, why don't you tell them about your drawing?" my dad hollered from behind us.

"I will, Dad!" I replied with a smile, feeling slightly embarrassed. We veered down a different path away from my parents. They headed up toward the event center.

"So, what is this drawing your dad mentioned?" Liz asked as we made our way through the sea of people.

"Oh, it's nothing," I could feel myself blushing.

"Come on Emily! It has to be *something!*" Ben pleaded.

"Okay okay! So, when I got home last night...I couldn't help but think about how I wished Halloween was still scary like it used to be. I started to daydream and think about the Spirit of Halloween, and what I think that might look like..."

"Aaand?" Liz inquired.

"So, I drew it. I gave it a giant pumpkin head, with swirl lollipop eyes, a gumdrop nose, and candy corn teeth…Really, it's nothing special." We made our way around a stable they used for a petting zoo.

"I mean it sounds really cool! I'd love to see it!" Ben answered. Butterflies filled my stomach, and I blushed.

"Okay! I'll bring it to school!"

We walked further down the path and watched as a truck with a gigantic pumpkin in the bed, drove toward the event center.

"Wow, the pumpkins just seem to get bigger and bigger every year," Liz commented. Ben and I agreed.

As the truck made its way past us, I looked off in the distance and saw a bunch of kids and teenagers forming around the nearby cornfield. My eyes grew wide when I saw a sign towering above all the kids. It read: **1st Annual Corn Maze.**

"Oh wow! Look!" I yelled, pointing at the cornfield.

"Oh cool! I bet we could get lost in there for hours!" Ben exclaimed.

We jogged over to the corn maze and waited in the short line.

As we entered the corn maze, we grabbed one of the maps from the bin at the entrance. The corn maze was in the shape of a skull, which I found very cool.

We made our way through the windy corn maze, ensuring we followed the map to a tee. It was creepy being in a narrow path between giant corn stalks. As the wind lightly blew, the corn stalks rustled against each other and made an ominous hissing noise.

The only thing I was bummed out about was the fact that the owners of Gantzler Farm didn't add in creepy Halloween decorations. Their decorations were just cartoony props periodically set along the path.

Finally, after what felt like an eternity, we made it down the final straightaway where we could see the exit.

"Look! We made it!" Liz exclaimed. We all ran toward the finish line.

As we drew nearer to the opening, I could hear what sounded like corn stalks crackling and snapping next to us.

"What was that?" Ben asked as we came to a screeching halt.

Everything grew silent. Then, straight ahead of us in the corn field... *snap...crunch...snap...crunch.*

Someone or *something* walked toward us.

"What *is* that?" Ben whispered.

"Shh!" I hissed as the noises began once again. *Snap...snap...crunch...crunch.*

I could feel my heart beating out of my chest as the suspense and anxiety began to build. Could it be a wild animal?

The noises now picked up a full head of steam...*Snap, snap, snap, crunch, snap*! It was heading straight for us at a furious pace!

8.

Before any of us could react, two terrifying zombie-like creatures came groaning and staggering toward us from the corn stalks.

Liz let out a horrified scream and Ben yelled, "Run!"

We turned and ran full sprint toward the exit until we heard raucous laughter bellowing from behind us.

We stopped at the exit and turned to see Bryce and Tyler standing in the middle of the path, their zombie masks lifted. They were both hunched over in laughter.

"Oh man, did you see the look on their faces?" Bryce choked out between breaths of laughter.

"Yeah, they *actually* thought we were zombies!" Tyler exclaimed.

"Suckers!" Bryce cried. Both erupted into hysterics once again.

I was so irritated. Normally I like being scared. If it was anyone other than them—or Sierra and Kelly--I'd have been laughing too.

"You guys are real jerks!" Liz yelled as we left the corn maze.

"I hate those guys," Ben admitted as we walked back toward the main part of the farm.

"Do you guys want to check out how the pumpkin carving contest is going?" I asked, trying to get our minds off those jerks, Bryce and Tyler.

"Yeah, that's cool," Ben said. He still sounded a little deflated after running away from Bryce and Tyler.

"It'll be fun! Come on! Forget those guys!"

"You know what? Yeah, forget them!" Ben cried in agreement.

We made our way toward the massive white tent that held the pumpkin carving contest where I was hoping to see some cool and creepy jack-o-lanterns. There were rows and rows of tables set up. Kids, teenagers, and adults alike were all busily carving away at their pumpkins.

There were a few neat witch, ghost, and monster designs. Most of which came from the adults. However, most of the jack-o-lanterns were just your standard faces being carved free-hand.

"Well, that was a little anti-climactic," Liz said as we exited the pumpkin carving tent.

"Yeah, no kidding," I agreed. "I remember when people would carve the scariest jack-o-lanterns I'd ever seen. It just feels like there is no passion anymore. Everything is just so cookie cutter."

I couldn't believe it. Was Halloween really becoming this mundane? Was there no passion around it anymore? Where did it go? Or maybe things were just *feeling* less scary now that we were starting to get older.

Either way, I just wished Halloween would go back to the way it used to feel. There's no way it was ever this silly when I was younger.

"Guess we should head up to the event center," Ben offered up. He sounded a little bit crushed.

"Yeah...guess so," I replied. "At least we'll still get to see a car get smashed. That's always fun!"

We made the long trek over to the event center, passing all the craft vendors and food trucks along the way.

At least the smell of the food trucks and the sight of the craft tables reminded me of the old days. That part hadn't changed.

We finally reached the event center. It was an extremely large pavilion with rows upon rows of bleachers facing a dirt pit. I glanced around. It was packed. Not one empty seat in the pavilion.

Ben, Liz and I stood along the outer fence so we could watch. The nice thing about Pumpkin Fest – was they did little shows and rodeos prior to the pumpkin weigh-ins so that people could enjoy what Pumpkin Fest had to offer before the main event.

I glanced around the dirt pit. There were a ton of enormous pumpkins resting on pallets, and a massive scale right in the center of it all.

"Holy cow!" Ben exclaimed.

"Right?" I said with a grin. Some things never get old.

An announcer walked out into the middle of the arena with a microphone in hand. The teams who'd brought the pumpkins came out and stood next to their prized possessions.

The announcer began to yell emphatically into his microphone to hype up the crowd.

"Welcome to the 23rd Annual Pumpkin Fest! Are you guys ready to weigh these behemoths or what?" he shouted. The crowd roared with cheering and whistles.

"Alright, you guys know the deal! The winning team will walk away with a $1,000 check and the honor of hoisting their pumpkin with the crane and dropping it onto the car afterward! Are y'all ready to go?" He yelled. The crowd roared even louder.

"Alright then! Ladies and gentlemen...without further ado! Let's hear it for our competitors!" A final cheer from the crowd greeted a forklift as it made its way out to the first pumpkin.

Country music played through the sound system while the forklift raised the pallet and pumpkin. It placed the pumpkin on the scale.

The whole event went by quickly. There were fourteen entrants this year, and these had to be the largest pumpkins I had ever seen.

The first few pumpkins came in between eight hundred and one thousand pounds. After that, the pumpkins slowly got heavier and heavier. With two pumpkins to go, the heaviest so far had been one thousand eight hundred and thirty-one pounds. The crowd was going insane!

The second-to last pumpkin didn't manage to knock the current champion off the leaderboard, coming in just shy at one thousand eight hundred and seventeen pounds, causing the crowd to murmur in shock.

Finally, the last pumpkin was lifted over to the scale. It appeared to be smaller than the current leader. It was a wide, flat pumpkin, resembling a pumpkin pancake, if there ever was such a thing. It was strange to see.

The forklift lowered the final pumpkin onto the scale. The crowd fell silent as the apprehension built.

"And ladies and gentlemen, we have a NEW champion! This giant weighed in at two thousand two hundred and forty-six pounds! Wow!" exclaimed the host. The crowd roared.

"Oh my god!" Ben exclaimed. "That thing weighs more than a ton!"

Liz and I were just as pleased as Ben. None of us thought that pumpkin would be that heavy. Clearly, looks were deceiving and we hadn't anticipated it being the heaviest one at all.

The host announced a short intermission while they cleared out all the pumpkins and brought in the car and crane to finish the event. The crowd buzzed with excitement. I mean, who doesn't enjoy watching a giant pumpkin get dropped on a car?

Time seemed to creep by. Finally, the crane came in. It carried the car into the pavilion from a gate opening. The crowd got up to their feet and began cheering as the car was placed at the center of the arena. A crew of workers unstrapped the car and then worked on getting the pumpkin strapped into the crane.

The giant pumpkin rose higher and higher until it reached the top point of the crane, much to the crowd's enjoyment.

The host came back out and hyped everyone up some more as the contest winner hopped up into the crane and received instructions.

"Alright, everyone. We're going to begin the countdown. Who's ready for a smashing good time?" He bounced around in an animated way, flailing his arms in the air and pointing around at everyone in the stands, and the crowd went crazy.

"Alright, here we go! 10, 9, 8, 7, 6, 5, 4, 3, 2, 1...AND GO!" The host yelled.

Immediately, the straps wrapped around the pumpkin snapped open, and the massive pumpkin began a freefall from at least 80 feet in the air. Time seemed to slow down as we watched the pumpkin slowly make its descent. Finally, it crash landed onto the old beat-up car, absolutely flattening it. Pumpkin chunks and guts flew everywhere.

It was a sight that never got old! Everyone, including me, erupted into boisterous cheers, providing the event crew with a standing ovation.

After the car crush ceremony, we met up with both Ben and Liz's parents. All of us agreed on food and had delicious barbecue from a food truck named *Big Brad's BBQ*. After we finished eating, we looked around at the craft vendors before going our separate ways.

I couldn't help but feel my spirits lift after the event was over and my parents and I returned home. All in all, it was a good day —aside from Bryce and Tyler being jerks and the non-spooky pumpkin carvings. Thankfully I hadn't had to deal with Sierra or Kelly. I was shocked we'd managed to elude them.

My parents and I capped off the night by playing a couple of board games before I went to bed. When they wished me goodnight, my dad promised they would start building my creation while I was at school the next day. I couldn't wait!

While lying in bed, unable to fall asleep, I found myself reminiscing about how Halloween used to be. Today was fun, but nothing about it was scary.

Just as I closed my eyes, I found myself thinking about my Spirit of Halloween. If only it could come to life and make Halloween scary again, that would be awesome. Maybe then people would treat the holiday as it was meant to be. I wanted it to happen so badly.

The sound of the howling wind whisked me away into a deep sleep once more.

The next morning, I felt off while getting ready for school. I felt slightly dizzy, almost like you do when you have a bad case of the flu. Other than that, I felt fine...just...off. I brushed it off as not sleeping well.

After getting dressed, I grabbed my drawing to show Ben and Liz at school. I wanted to see what they thought about it. The more I looked at it, the more I loved it. I couldn't wait for my mom and dad to build it as a Halloween prop for our yard.

I could tell my mom was excited when she dropped me off,. She worked at the museum part-time and was off today. She seemed eager to work on building my Halloween idea.

"Have a good day at school!" she yelled as I left the car and went inside.

I managed to find Liz waiting by my locker. She and I made small talk while we waited for Ben, who hurried over to us a couple of minutes later.

"Hey guys!" he shouted as he ran over.

"Now who's late?" I joked.

Ben could only grin and shake his head.

"Emily was just about to show me her drawing," Liz declared, folding her arms.

"Oh cool! I was afraid I was going to miss it!" Ben replied.

Ben's class schedule was different from ours. For some reason, our school decided to break lunch into two periods starting this year, and Ben didn't share the same lunch time as Liz and me. We didn't have any classes together either, unfortunately.

"Nope, you made it just in time," I said with a smile. I pulled the drawing out of my purse and showed it to them.

Ben and Liz's eyes grew wide with excitement.

"That is SO COOL!" Ben exclaimed. Liz grabbed the drawing from my hands.

"Oh my god, Emily, this is so detailed and so good!" Liz said.

"Thanks, guys. I don't know why this thought came into my head, but it did, and I am really proud of it. I guess my mom and dad are going to the hobby store today to get the stuff to build it!"

"That is such an awesome idea!" Liz replied. "I can't wait to see how it turns out!"

Before I could respond to Liz, we were interrupted by a familiar voice I'd hoped I wouldn't hear.

"What 'cha guys lookin' at?" Sierra said. She reached over, snatched the drawing out of Liz's hands, and scanned it and then showed it to Kelly, Bryce, and Tyler.

"Don't worry about it!" I yelled as I reached for the drawing, but Sierra quickly pulled it away and handed it over to her boyfriend Bryce.

"What the heck is it?" Sierra asked as she and her friends gawked at my sketch.

"It's my drawing, give it back," I demanded.

"It looks goofy," Bryce called out in his bumbling oafish voice.

"Says you," Ben replied.

"Quiet down, weasel," Tyler called out. He shoved Ben backward. He hit the locker behind him with a crash.

"Look, just give it back!" Liz pleaded.

"What's its name? Johnny Pumpkinseed?" Bryce croaked.

"Give it back," Ben said. He marched forward and shoved Bryce.

Suddenly, a scuffle between Ben and Bryce broke out. A teacher, Mr. Bradford, ran over to break it up. Mr. Bradford was a tall and skinny history teacher. He had short curly black hair, thin glasses and always wore dress shirts with khaki pants.

"What's going on here?" Mr. Bradford asked as he separated Ben and Bryce.

"They took my drawing and wouldn't give it back. Ben was sticking up for me," I said. I shot a dirty look at Sierra and her group of friends.

During the scuffle, Bryce had dropped my drawing on the floor. Mr. Bradford bent down and handed it back to me and then told all of us to head to class.

The way Sierra and her friends treated my drawing and made fun of it really upset me. I'd worked hard on it and thought it was super cool and creepy. Bryce's calling it "Johnny Pumpkinseed" really made me angry. It robbed the monster of its scariness and made it feel like a cartoon.

I wanted nothing more than to go home and see how far along my parents were with making my vision a reality.

10.

When my mom picked me up from school, she told me, much to my dismay, that she and my dad had agreed not to show me the project until it was finished.

The whole rest of the week dragged on after that. Every day I would come home from school and find it unfinished. Tuesday, it wasn't finished. Wednesday, it wasn't finished. Thursday, same thing.

Finally, it was Friday. I guess Bryce decided to fight Ben during second lunch that day and Ben got a black eye. Both boys were given detention instead of a suspension.

Our school views first-time offenses as something that shouldn't take students away from school. Instead, they'd torture you by keeping you after school for a couple of hours, especially with it being Friday. I felt terrible for Ben. The only reason he was in this mess was because he stood up for me.

I told my mom about it as we drove home. She seemed visibly upset. "I'm sorry you have to deal with bullies, honey. I promise, it doesn't last forever."

"It's okay Mom," I said calmly. "You and Dad have raised me to be better than the bullies."

Mom smiled. As we turned down the street which led to our house, I noticed something in our front yard. It was covered with a sheet.

"Mom...what's that?" I asked, my heart skipping a few beats.

"We finished your design," she said with a huge smile.

"Oh, my goodness! This is so awesome! I can't wait to see it!"

As soon as Mom parked in our driveway, I immediately unbuckled my seatbelt and bolted out of the car. My dad stood proudly at attention in the front yard, hands on his hips, a broad smile across his face.

"Well?" I asked as I came sprinting over.

They had covered the prop in a sheet so I couldn't see it until they unveiled it. It stood directly behind the cemetery, and looked to be at least seven or eight feet tall.

"Are you ready?" my dad asked, gripping the sheet draped over the top of it.

"Yes!" I had been waiting all week. I couldn't remember being this excited about something for a long time.

"Alright then!" he said and ripped the sheet away, revealing an exact replica of my vision.

I walked closer to it. It was massive. Its pumpkin head was huge and super detailed. They had nailed every single aspect, from the long curly stem atop his head, to the red and white swirl lollipop eyes and green gumdrop nose. Dad had even carved a jack-o-lantern grin into the foam, and inserted candy corn teeth into its smile as well.

They'd done a fantastic job with the paint. Even up close, you would swear it was a real pumpkin, with real candy. They even managed to make the green gumdrop nose look like it had sugar sprinkled all over it. And his hands. His fingers! They were just the way I'd drawn them!

"It's perfect!" I cried.

"Well, we're glad you love it, Emily. Thank you for inspiring us. I really think this is going to win the best yard contest this year," Dad replied. He sounded extremely proud, which made me feel great.

I ran over and gave them both a hug. Then I turned back to look at it one more time. They'd even managed to find a black-and-white flannel shirt, blue jeans, and boots big enough for this monstrous creation.

"Where did you find the clothes?" I asked with a chuckle.

"Big and tall section at the store," my dad replied with a laugh.

"Come on inside Ronnie, we'll start getting dinner ready," my mom said, as she tugged my dad away. I stayed so I could enjoy my creation alone for a little bit.

I walked back over to the giant rendition of my drawing my parents had put together, staring at it in total admiration.

"You're *not* Johnny Pumpkinseed," I said, as if the prop could understand me. "You're too scary for that. No, you're more of a...more of a Johnny Rotten...Yeah, that sounds more like it!"

I did a circle around the prop and looked up into its lollipop eyes.

"I wish you were real. I wish you could come to life at night and pay back the bullies for always picking on me. They think you look stupid. I think you look awesome. I just *wish* you would bring the scary back to Halloween."

I stood back for a moment, waiting for him to spring to life.

"What am I thinking? Of course, you aren't going to come alive. I am losing my mind," I whispered to myself.

I was about to walk inside, when I thought I saw one of Johnny Rotten's fingers twitch. When I looked back, however, they were in the same position they'd been in before.

I shook my head and whispered to myself, "Get a grip, Emily."

11.

My mom was called into work to help prepare for an event at the museum, leaving me and my dad alone. We were sitting on the couch, watching one of our favorite sitcoms, when he turned to me and said, "Hey, why don't you call Ben and Liz and see if they want to go to Zappy's tonight?"

Zappy's was a haunted hayride just outside of town that operated every Halloween season. This was going to be its seventh year and, supposedly, it's most frightening yet.

"Really?" I asked him, a little shocked. Usually, we went to haunted houses closer to Halloween.

"Yeah, it beats sitting here on the couch watching TV. Your mom won't be home 'til late anyhow," he replied.

"Okay!" I yelled gleefully. and I hopped up off the couch to call Ben and Liz.

I called Ben's house first, but his mom answered the phone. She informed me, in a very annoyed tone, that Ben had been grounded and wasn't going anywhere. I apologized to her and hung up.

"Ben can't come," I yelled to Dad.

I called Liz's house next. She was on board with joining us and just as excited as I was. We both loved going to Zappy's every year.

"Can Liz stay the night?" I hollered from the kitchen.

"That's fine," Dad yelled back. "We'll head over to pick her up in a little bit."

I could hardly contain my excitement as I hung up the phone.

I bounded my way through the living room to head upstairs to my room. I needed to find my favorite Halloween hoodie. It was orange and had vintage Halloween art all over it with an old black cat, jack-o-lanterns, spiders and spiderwebs, as well as witches and skulls.

I was elated. Liz hadn't been over for a sleepover since summer break. To top it off, we were going to our favorite haunted hayride!

After changing into my hoodie and a pair of black jeans, I quickly scurried down the steps. Dad had on his normal clothing. He wore a plain grey t-shirt under a red long-sleeved flannel jacket, blue jeans and a pair of boots.

"Ready to roll?" He asked with a grin as I slid on my favorite white sneakers.

"Yep! Are you ready to scream like a little girl?"

"Oh! Is that what you think is going to happen? Okay, we'll see how that works out for you," He laughed as he held our side door open for me.

Dad and I have always been very close, and we crack jokes on one another every time an opportunity presents itself.

As we pulled down the driveway, I looked up at Johnny Rotten. I smiled and waved at him. "Bye, Johnny Rotten!"

"Johnny Rotten?" Dad asked, glancing at me.

"Yeah, that's what I decided to name him."

"Oh, I see...I think that's the perfect name for him!"

A couple of minutes later, we pulled up in front of Liz's house. My dad laid on his horn a couple of times to let Liz know we were there.

I rolled my window down while we waited. It was another picturesque early fall evening in northern Georgia. The sun was setting, but it was still warm outside. A light, calming early fall breeze blew as orange light from the falling sun cascaded over the neighborhood.

Liz finally came bursting through the front door of her house. Her arms were full and she struggled to make her way to the car. She had a backpack over her back, a sleeping bag in one arm, and a pillow in the other.

My dad pressed a button to open the back of the SUV for her. She gratefully placed her stuff inside before shutting it all in.

"Hey Liz!" my dad exclaimed as she hopped into the car and buckled herself in.

"Hey Mr. Riggs!"

I could tell she was every bit as excited as I was.

"Liz, who do you think is going to scream first? Me or Emily?" Dad asked as we pulled away from her house.

There was a moment of silence. I looked over at Liz, who seemed to be mulling over the decision.

"Hmm...I gotta go with you, Mr. Riggs!" Liz said.

Dad's reaction was priceless. His eyes grew wide as his jaw dropped and he let out a disgusted sound of mock surprise which caused Liz and me to erupt into laughter.

"I'll remember that when a zombie or werewolf comes to get you girls. I'll let them take you both!"

"No, no, no!" Liz cried, laughing. "I change my answer! I think Emily will be the one screaming!"

"It's too late for that. You made your bed, now you have to lie in it," my dad said.

I glanced over at Liz and faked a hurt expression. "I can't believe you!"

"Sorry, I'm not about to be zombie food," she replied, causing all of us to laugh.

Through all the fun and excitement, we finally arrived at the farm where Zappy's Haunted Hayride was held. The only parking available was in the grassy part of the yard and it was already packed. The sun was now nearly gone, and darkness was beginning to creep in.

I couldn't wait.

12.

As we walked from the car to the entrance, I felt something touch my neck from behind. I almost jumped out of my shoes when I turned around and saw an actor dressed up as a ghoul standing right behind us.

"RAHH!" The actor yelled, sending a jolt of fear through my entire body.

I couldn't help letting out a scream.

"Told you," my dad joked as we continued toward the entrance.

"Whatever," I replied, slightly embarrassed as he and Liz laughed at my expense.

Zappy's was one of the few haunted attractions I knew of that allowed its actors to touch you. I knew deep down that they were actors, and I was never *actually* going to be in danger. There was just something about people dressed up as monsters grabbing you that added to the already heightened fear.

The front entrance had a giant sign with yellow lights shining at it that read *Zappy's Haunted Hayride.* The whole area had a tall wooden fence around it, so you couldn't see inside and had to go through the main gate.

Right as we crossed the barrier of the entrance, a figure dressed up as a deranged farmer lunged at Liz and me, screaming as he did so.

Liz and I jumped back and shrieked in fright.

"Dang it!" I yelled, as my dad once again burst into laughter.

"I hate you, Mr. Riggs," Liz choked out. My dad laughed even harder as she tried to catch her breath.

"Aww! I know," he replied, his voice oozing with sarcasm as we continued down the path to the ticket booth.

Dad paid for our tickets to go through the hayride. The lady running the booth instructed us to continue down the pathway until we hit the line and told us to have an extra spooky night.

There was just something about the fall air and going to haunted attractions that I truly loved, and I know it was the same for Liz and my dad as well.

The show must have already begun, because we could hear the screams of terrified guests making their way through the horrifying hayride.

Occasionally, a chainsaw was revved up, accompanied by distant screams as well. It was so exhilarating. Even waiting in line was a treat.

The line moved really slow, but we kept ourselves entertained by joking around and watching the actors as they scared unsuspecting guests who ran away in fright.

"This place is awesome, isn't it girls?" Dad asked as his eyes surveyed around the area.

We both looked up at him, smiled and nodded our heads in agreement.

Suddenly, something grabbed both Liz and me from behind. We let out startled yelps as we turned to see a demented old farmer with repulsive makeup laughing and snarling at us. We both tried to pull our arms away, but he wouldn't let go!

"No! No! You can have them!" my dad joked.

"Oh? Is that so?" The farmer asked in a snarly, scratchy voice. He yanked on our arms, drawing us toward him.

"Yep. They thought I'd be scared and screaming before them," Dad said, grinning.

"Tsk tsk tsk...now you girls are mine!" the farmer yelled. He let out a maniacal laugh.

"Let us go!" Liz screamed as she tugged at her arm, trying to free herself.

I tried to do the same, but the farmer's grip tightened. I became legitimately fearful for my life.

"Come on! Let go!" I howled.

The old farmer snarled "No!"

As soon as that word left his mouth, Liz and I managed to escape his grasp. The old farmer let out a sinister chuckle as he waddled away from us.

My dad was roaring with laughter at this point. I gave him a punch on the arm.

"What?" he chuckled, throwing his arms up.

As soon as he said this, an actor came up behind him, dressed as a clown. The actor raised a blowhorn and set it off right behind my dad's head. I had never seen my dad jump that high from a scare in my life! He flew over by Liz and me, letting out a frightened yelp of his own. He hunched over, clutching at his chest and it was our turn to return the favor and laugh at him.

"Good lord. That almost gave me a heart attack," he said as he stood upright and took a deep breath.

"Oh, that was great!" I yelled.

"How does it feel?" Liz added.

"Yeah, yeah! Point proven," Dad said. "Truce?" He stretched his hand out to shake ours.

"Fine. Truce," we said. We each took a turn shaking his hand.

"Teamwork makes the dream work," he said, as the line moved forward. We were finally going to get on the hayride. Screams and yells continued to pierce the night sky as we eagerly awaited our tractor to arrive.

"Here it comes!" Dad exclaimed.

Liz and I tried to stand on our tiptoes to see the tractor pulling up, but we were too short. I guess it pays to be tall like my dad.

Moments later, the large tractor came rumbling past us and the wagon in the back stopped directly in front of our group.

"All aboard!" The man driving the tractor yelled. The lady standing by our group lifted the rope and we proceeded through the entrance to find our seats on the wagon.

Liz and I rushed to the front, facing the line we'd just left. Our backs would be to the dark and foreboding farmland behind us. Dad popped a squat next to us and everyone else found their way to a seat of their own.

I noticed something as I stared back at the crowd of people waiting in line. My heart skipped a beat, my stomach sank, and my brain was sent into a whirlwind of confusion.

Standing on the outskirts of the crowd, under a dimly lit pole was Johnny Rotten. It was him to a tee. Right down to the lollipop eyes and leafy hands. I couldn't believe my eyes.

"Dad! Dad!" I yelled, tugging at his shirt sleeve.

"What, hon?"

"Look!" I pointed back out toward the sea of people. "It's Johnny Rotten!"

"What are you talking about Emily?"

I looked back to the place where Johnny Rotten had been standing just seconds ago. He was gone!

"He was over there, Dad! I swear he was!"

"Honey, you probably just saw an actor with a mask on. That's all," Dad replied calmly as the tractor engine fired back up.

"No, he even had the lollipop swirl eyes! Dad, it was him!"

"Come on Emily, that isn't possible. It is made of foam and latex. It's not a real person," he replied.

I let out a sigh. Maybe Dad was right. Maybe it was all in my head. My imagination must have gotten the best of me. Liz sat beside me in awkward silence.

"Uh...who's Johnny Rotten?" she finally asked.

"That's what Emily named the Halloween decoration we made from her drawing," Dad replied.

"Gotcha," Liz said. "Relax Emily, your dad is right. It's just a prop."

"It was probably just an actor," I admitted woefully.

There was a moment of silence before the man driving the tractor honked his horn and we began moving.

"Yeehaw!" The man exclaimed. "Thank you all for joining us at Zappy's Haunted Hayride. As some of you may know, Arthur Zappy built this farm. But it was no ordinary farm mind you. No! This farm didn't raise animals or grow crops," he paused, allowing the suspense to build.

"No, Mr. Zappy built this farm to house the scariest, craziest, and most frightening monsters and creatures known to man. Always keep all arms and legs inside the wagon if you want to keep 'em that way.

"And one other thing. Enjoy the ride!" He yelled before busting out a crazy laugh.

Everyone on the wagon cheered as we made our way toward the main entrance of the haunt. My heart beat faster with anticipation and excitement.

"Man, they've really upped the scare factor this year!" my dad proclaimed. Another dad who'd come with his family, gave my dad a fist bump in agreement.

Our tractor made its way through the wooded area. We were coming up on a big black sheet that blocked everything from our line of sight. We were shrouded in darkness until we crossed to the other side.

As soon as we did, loud creepy music blared, and all these crazy deformed farmers ran up to the wagon, wielding chainsaws and howling at us. They ran the chainsaws along the wagon and occasionally ran the whining saws against one of the guests.

Everyone on our wagon was either screaming or laughing as we continued through the ride.

Next up, we came up on an area of zombies who began attacking our wagon. One of them grabbed onto my wrist and pretended to bite me. I wailed as I yanked my arm away. Dad was smiling from ear to ear, so I shot him a dirty look.

We drove through a circus tent filled with psycho clowns wielding axes and other weapons next. They came up to the wagon and beat on it aggressively as they wailed and belted out their creepy clown laughs.

We had an absolute blast as the tractor continued to meander through the maze-like path in the woods. We drove past a few giant animatronics. One was a *huge* dragon that blew fire from up above.

We finished the hayride with some of the more classic areas where werewolves, mud people, and other ominous creatures ran amok.

We tried to keep tally on who had been scared the most, but lost track about halfway through the ride. Liz had been in the lead before we could no longer keep count.

All in all, we all got scared and had fun at the same time. It was just the kind of night I needed. In the back of my mind though, I couldn't help but think back to what I'd seen. Did I really see Johnny Rotten? If so, how was that possible?

The more I thought about it, the more I realized it wasn't my imagination. I knew what I saw, and it was Johnny Rotten.

14.

When we finally made it home, and were pulling up our driveway, I pointed toward our front yard.

"See, that's Johnny Rotten," I told Liz.

"Ooh! Can we go look at him?"

"Absolutely," Dad answered as he parked the car.

Mom's car was already in the driveway, so Dad grabbed Liz's stuff from the back of the car and went inside. Liz and I visited Johnny Rotten out front.

This was my first time seeing him lit up by our Halloween lights. He looked even scarier under the dim green and orange lighting. Something appeared off though.

"Oh man, this thing is *so* creepy!" Liz shouted. "It's perfect!"

"Yeah, but something seems...*off*.".

"What do you mean?"

I examined Johnny Rotten's position. "I mean it doesn't look like he is standing the same way he was before." He seemed to be standing in the same place, but *something* seemed different, and I couldn't quite put my finger on it.

"Oh, come on, Emily. It's probably just the way the lighting is hitting it," Liz scoffed.

I cocked my head at an angle, still trying to figure it out. "Yeah, maybe you're right. Let's head inside."

Inside, we found my mom standing in the kitchen making snacks. She greeted us warmly and gave us both hugs.

"It's so good to see you again, Liz!" Mom said.

"Where's Dad?" I asked.

"He took Liz's stuff up to your room. He's probably still upstairs.,"

Liz and I headed through the kitchen and into the living room. When we entered the living room, my dad lunged out and scared both of us.

He couldn't contain his laughter as Liz and I jumped back and screamed.

"I can't believe you!" I shouted. We both gave him a playful shove before hurrying upstairs to unpack Liz's belongings.

When we came back downstairs, my mom and dad were in the kitchen. Mom brought chips and dip into the living room along with a bowl of popcorn.

"Your father said the living room is for you girls tonight. You can pick any horror movie as long as it's PG-13 or less," Mom said as she placed the snacks on the coffee table.

"Oh! What to choose. What to choose!" I said as Liz and I moved to the entertainment stand that housed all our DVD's.

"Have fun tonight girls," Dad said as he entered the living room. He set a can of soda for each of us on the coffee table. "Your mother has to be up early tomorrow for work, so please keep the noise levels down."

"Okay! Goodnight Mom. Goodnight Dad," I said. I ran over and gave them both hugs.

"Goodnight Mr. and Mrs. Riggs," Liz said, continuing her scan through our collection of movies.

"Goodnight girls," Mom said.

"Stay out of trouble...and watch out for *ghooouls*," Dad said in his best spooky voice.

"HA!" Liz pretended to laugh.

My mom gave Dad a smack on his arm and they marched upstairs.

"Did you find anything you want to watch?" I asked Liz.

"How about this?" Liz pointed at a movie on the shelf.

"Ooh! *The Haunting at Run Road...excellent* choice," I said, sliding the movie into our Blu-Ray player.

We went upstairs and changed into our pajamas while the previews played. When we came back downstairs, the main menu was on the screen.

Liz and I each grabbed a blanket and snacked on the food and drinks my parents had left us while the movie played.

The movie was about a group of teenagers who ventured out into farm country to a house on Run Road. Apparently, a witch lived and died in the home and had continued to haunt it to this day.

The movie was packed with great jump scares which kept Liz and me on the edge of our seats throughout. By the time the movie had ended, we were both spooked.

Every time the house made a creak, or a pipe clattered, we jumped out of our skin and tried to convince ourselves that it was nothing.

Finally, we managed to fall asleep on the couches in the living room.

Sometime in the middle of the night, I woke to a loud noise. It sounded like a tree branch snapping, followed by a loud *thud* out in the front yard.

I woke up in a frightened daze and looked over at Liz. She was sound asleep. Everything fell silent once again. My heart raced. I felt delirious as though I'd just been woken up out of a deep sleep.

Suddenly, I heard footsteps on our front porch. The footsteps slowly moved toward our front door. My breathing got heavier and heavier as I sat completely frozen on the couch.

Then, the door handle jiggled, as if someone were trying to come inside. I couldn't move. I couldn't scream. All I could do was sit on the couch, paralyzed with fear as my heart pounded away furiously.

Things fell silent once again and remained silent for what felt like an eternity.

Finally, I grew calm and started thinking. What struck me as odd was the fact that I never heard footsteps *leaving* the front porch.

After several minutes, I finally mustered enough courage to check outside.

I slowly and quietly tip-toed toward the window.

In the blink of an eye, I heard loud thunderous footsteps pounding quickly across the porch again, this time away from the door. I let out a frightened gasp at the sound of the heavy boots.

I inched forward to the window and ripped open the blinds to look outside. There was no one on the porch and no one in sight. I continued to survey around and noticed everything was in order. The skeletons were still playing cards at the table on our porch, and I could see Johnny Rotten's pumpkin head from the window, standing in his usual spot.

"What was that?" I whispered to myself, still feeling freaked out.

I didn't know what to think or what to make of it. Was it the horror movie that made me imagine things like earlier? I know what footsteps sound like, and my mind couldn't possibly be making that up.

What could it have been though? *Think Emily. Think.*

The only logical explanations I could come up with was that it was either me being delirious from a dream, or that it was an animal. Nothing else made any sense. Otherwise, wouldn't Liz have heard the same thing and woken up as well?

That was one of the scariest moments in my entire life. However, I finally managed to fall back to sleep after tossing and turning for what felt like an eternity.

15.

Thump. Thump. Thump. Thump. Footsteps jolted me awake again, this time coming from inside the house. I sat bolt upright in fright. I looked over just as my dad came down the staircase.

"Jeez! You scared me, Dad!" I whispered hoarsely, trying not to wake Liz, who was still snoozing on the opposite couch.

It shocked me that I never heard my mom come downstairs when she left in the morning. She must have been extremely careful and quiet when she left.

"Sorry!" he whispered back. "Are you hungry?"

Before I could answer, Liz woke as well. She sat up, yawned and stretched.

"Good morning, sunshines!" Dad said, all bright-eyed and bushy-tailed, as if he hadn't just rudely woken me up fifteen seconds ago.

"Good morning Mr. Riggs," Liz grunted, stretching again.

"How'd you two sleep last night?" he asked.

"I slept like a baby," Liz said, tossing her blanket aside.

"I didn't sleep well at all last night," I admitted. "I woke up to footsteps on our front porch."

"Footsteps?" Dad and Liz asked at the same time.

"Yes, and then I heard the doorknob start jiggling as if someone were trying to get in," I said with a shudder.

"And you didn't think to wake me up?" Dad asked

"It's fine, Dad. I went over to the window to look and there was no one out there. It must have been a nightmare or something," I said, but I still felt unsure of what might've happened.

"Well, alright then. I'm just glad it was a dream," he said. "Are you girls hungry? I'm going to make some scrambled eggs and bacon."

"That sounds awesome!" shouted Liz. She got up off the couch and hurried to the bathroom.

"Yeah Dad, that's fine," I said glumly, as he walked into the kitchen to start breakfast.

I was feeling a little out of whack again this morning. I hadn't slept well at all. I just felt tired, and a little woozy. My anxiety was still in overdrive from last night too.

I just need to get up and get moving.

I heard my dad turn on the small TV in the kitchen while he cooked our breakfast. He'd turned on the local news.

I poured myself a glass of orange juice as the news lady begin speaking.

"News out of Buford this morning. There are several reports coming in, from around the city, of a man in pumpkin mask scaring children…" My dad walked over to the TV and turned up the volume as Liz joined us in the kitchen.

"…The man was wearing a flannel shirt and had a pumpkin mask on. Reports state that he was seen staring into windows of several homes throughout the night, going so far as to bang on one child's window," They quickly cut to a video interview with the child.

"It was terrifying," the little boy said, tears welling up in his eyes. "He came right up to my bedroom window and just started pounding. When I went to get my parents, and we came back…he was gone!"

The report then cut to the parents talking about how upset they were and how they couldn't believe an adult would stoop so low as to scare children like that. They went on to say that the Pumpkin Man may have painted *HAPPY HALLOWEEN* on their garage door in red paint.

The video cut to show the vandalism.

"Wow. That's crazy!" Dad said in disbelief as he scooped eggs and bacon onto our plates.

"Right? Like, who does that?" Liz asked. She grabbed a glass of juice and sat at the table while my dad served her.

"Sometimes even adults can be jerks," Dad replied, handing me my plate and placing one in front of his seat as well.

I sat in silence. My stomach was in absolute knots and my heart was racing. What if it was this man I'd heard out in front of our house? What if it was Johnny Rotten?

No...it couldn't be. But they did mention a pumpkin head. I didn't know what to think.

"Emily...Emily!" my dad said, snapping me out of my daydream. "Are you okay?"

"Y-yeah! Sorry, I just zoned out," I replied. I began eating my breakfast.

16.

After we finished breakfast, my dad said he'd like to head back up to Geno's. He wanted to get more decorations for the yard.

"Can Liz come with us?" I begged.

"That's fine, honey," Dad replied while he finished washing the dishes. "We can drop her off at home afterward,"

Liz and I rushed upstairs to change and get her stuff together.

Dad decided to shower and get ready before we left. So, Liz and I went out on the back deck to hang out and soak in the warm early morning sun while we waited.

We were having fun and talking when I heard a strange noise. I cut Liz off in the middle of her sentence.

"Shh," I hissed placing a finger to my lips.

Liz and I listened intently. Two voices filled the air. They were coming from our front yard. I motioned to Liz, and we crept off the porch to check it out.

As we moved around the side of the house, the voices grew clearer.

The voices belonged to Sierra and Kelly! What were they doing here?

I peeked around the corner of the house and saw them standing in front of Johnny Rotten.

"God, this thing is so hideous," Sierra commented.

"Right? Do they really think *this* is going to be enough to beat you guys?" Kelly joked.

Sierra and Kelly both snorted in derision and started giggling.

"Bryce was right. Johnny Pumpkinseed is super lame," Sierra snickered.

I had heard enough.

"Hey!" I cried, marching from around the corner. "What are you two doing here?"

They flinched at the sound of my voice, and then shot a disgusted look in our direction as Liz and I continued toward them.

"Just looking at your stupid decoration," Sierra spat.

"Oh yeah? At least it's an original, unlike all your store-bought junk!" I replied angrily.

"Whatever. I guess we'll see what the committee thinks next weekend," Sierra sneered. "Come on Kelly, let's get out of here."

"Emily...that was awesome!" Liz said, laughing heartily, as Sierra and Kelly stomped back across the street.

"What?"

"You told them off. That was great!"

"I just wish they would leave us alone," I replied. I looked up at Johnny Rotten.

My mind must've been playing tricks on me. I could've sworn his arm was at a different angle yesterday.

It had to be the lack of sleep.

17.

The three of us made our return trip to Geno's. On the way there, Dad said I could get my costume if I wanted to. This added a little pep to my step. There were going to be so many options!

"Alright, girls, just meet me over by the animatronics in about thirty minutes," Dad said. He pushed his cart out of sight.

I looked over at Liz, "Thirty minutes? I guess we're going to have to make this work!"

And with that, we both worked like busy bees, scouring through the costume section. Nothing really jumped out at me until we began surveying the wall of masks. There was a mask there that looked like a porcelain doll's face. It had cracks and chips in it.

My eyes grew wide with excitement.

"Ooh!" I exclaimed, reaching up and pulling the mask down.

"That is...horrifying," Liz said with a laugh.

"It's perfect! And I saw the perfect dress for it over here!"

We quickly walked to the aisle where I found an old-fashioned blue dress with a white fringe on it. It also came with white pantyhose and white gloves.

"And I'm done," I said triumphantly.

"That costume is absolutely terrifying," Liz replied raising an eyebrow.

"I know. It's going to be awesome. What are you going to be for Halloween?"

Liz pondered this for a second. "I was thinking of dressing up as a princess."

I looked at Liz and said, half-joking, "Hyuhh! Liz, you can't!"

Liz smiled, "You didn't let me finish. I was going to say ...a zombie princess."

I thought about it for a second and nodded in approval. "You know what, that would be amazing! But you could have been a regular princess if you wanted. I was only kidding."

"I know." She laughed. "Let's go find your dad."

18.

Dad had decided to buy a few vampire bat props from Geno's. He wanted to hang them from the front porch to tie everything together.

"Sounds cool, Dad!" I exclaimed, admiring the costume I had picked out. Dad was ecstatic when he saw the costume I'd come up with and told me he loved it. After dropping Liz off, Dad and I had to run and pick up a few pumpkins for carving. Halloween was still a couple weeks away, but the committee would be voting on the best yards next weekend and Dad said if we smeared petroleum jelly on our jack-o-lanterns, they would stay fresh longer.

After we returned to the house, I rushed inside while Dad pulled out the pumpkins and set up the vampire bat props on our front porch.

He had just finished up when I came back. The bats looked really cool. They were a couple feet long, and very detailed. He'd hung the three of them up sporadically across the gutters and it rounded out our decorating for the yard to perfection.

Dad took a step back and nodded in approval.

"This is our year, honey," he said as he went inside.

I couldn't help but agree. Everything looked creepy, especially at night.

I walked over to Johnny Rotten. He towered over me, his big pumpkin head shining brightly in the early evening sunlight.

"Was it you going around terrorizing the neighborhood?" I asked, hoping for some sort of answer.

Nothing happened. Johnny Rotten stood as still as a rock. I frowned slightly.

"Listen, if you are real, can you just give me a sign?" I asked.

Nothing.

"Great," I whispered. "I am losing my mind."

When I walked away, I noticed a small red splat mark on the steps leading to our front porch. I couldn't remember it being there before. I thought about this morning's newsbreak and the words *Happy Halloween* painted in red on that family's garage door.

I quickly turned back to Johnny, who remained as still as ever. *Nope. Just forget it, Emily.*

"Weird..." I muttered before heading inside.

I decided I'd had enough. My dad stood in the kitchen. He'd laid down some newspapers on the dinner table so we could carve our pumpkins.

"Mom is going to be home any minute," he said as he brought the three pumpkins over and placed them on the table. "Pick out whichever carving you want to do, and we'll start scooping the guts out."

He tossed over a couple of pumpkin carving books he'd bought at Geno's. Some people preferred to free hand their carvings. We preferred to get the pattern books, because they had the best designs.

Every year, since I was a little kid, people had come from all over Buford to look at our jack-o-lanterns.

I combed through the different patterns in the book. The patterns were sorted based on difficulty level. Usually, I would do easy or moderate level carvings. This year, I really wanted to push myself and try one of the difficult patterns.

I found an intricate zombie design and told dad it was the one I wanted to do.

"Are you sure?" he asked.

"Yep!" I replied fearlessly.

"Alright then," He grinned as he cut the page out and made the necessary slits in it before taping it to my pumpkin.

Dad wound up picking a vampire design and taped his page on his pumpkin as well.

"We'll let Mom pick hers when she gets home," Dad said, as we cut the tops off the pumpkins and scooped all the guts out.

Seeing all the pumpkin guts sprawled on the table reminded me of how I wished Johnny Rotten could puke pumpkin guts on kids who didn't respect Halloween. I couldn't help but smile at the thought. Maybe it was evil of me, or *maybe* those kids deserved it.

Just as we'd finished scooping out all three of the pumpkins, Mom came walking in the door. She gave us both a hug, said she was going to shower and would be down in a little bit. She'd pick her pattern out and start carving then.

A couple hours later, we had all three pumpkins carved and placed on our front porch steps. My zombie, my dad's vampire, and the cemetery design that my mom had picked out.

Dad placed candles inside each and lit them. We stood back as he plugged in the lighting for the decorations, as well as the fog machines. Dad came rushing over right after.

It was a sight to see. Everything looked perfect. So creepy, but so cool. Between Johnny Rotten and all our other props—the cemetery, the lighting, and the jack-o-lanterns with the fog rolling in...it looked fantastic!

We were all left speechless.

"This is what it's all about," my dad said, with a look of pride. "Come on, let's head inside and order some food."

The rest of the night was great. We ordered pizza from our favorite place and played a board game before settling in to watch one of our favorite family Halloween movies.

I love Halloween so much. It truly is the best time of the year.

19.

That night, I fell right to sleep. After no sleep the night before, and a pretty eventful day, I was worn out.

At some point in the middle of the night, I woke to a loud noise outside our house. It had sounded like clanking metal. Half-awake, and heart racing, I staggered over to my bedroom window.

In the ambient light from our Halloween decorations out front, I saw a shadow dart across the driveway and toward the front yard.

My eyes grew wide, and a shot of adrenaline coursed through my veins as I headed downstairs. My heart was absolutely pounding. I didn't know what I'd seen or what I'd heard, but I knew someone, or *something* was outside.

I was at the bottom of our staircase when I heard loud bootsteps running away from the front door once again. I ran as fast as I could to the front window and looked outside. To my amazement, I saw Johnny Rotten's head moving.

I could hardly breathe and my whole body was shaking. How could it be possible? I slowly made my way to the front door, unlocked it and stepped out barefoot onto the cold hardwood porch. I crept down the steps to look at Johnny Rotten.

He stood completely still, as strong winds whipped across the yard. The wind blew so hard, it caused him to wobble slightly.

My mind raced. Could the wind have moved Johnny Rotten's head? I looked toward our driveway. That wouldn't explain the shadow I saw running across it.

I walked to the driveway and noticed our metal trash bin had been knocked over.

"Must be the wind and my eyes playing tricks on me," I whispered to myself. I lifted the trash can up and placed it back where it belonged as another gust of wind tore through the crisp night air.

"What are you doing out here?" I heard my dad yell from behind me. He stood in the doorway of the house. It caught me completely off guard and I let out a gasp of fright.

"Dad, you scared me!" I cried.

"Scared you? I heard footsteps on our staircase and got up to see our front door wide open. You want to talk about being scared?"

"I'm sorry, Dad," I replied, lowering my gaze to the ground. "I-I heard a noise out here and thought I saw something, so I came out to check…"

"Well, next time come get me if that happens," he replied sternly as I made my way back up to the porch. "You never know what kinda crazies are out there."

After that, Dad tucked me in. My alarm clock read a little after three in the morning.

When he left and shut my door, my brain wandered through the events that had taken place. The wind could explain everything *except* the shadow that ran past our driveway. I still couldn't wrap my mind around that part. Was it Johnny Rotten? Or was it the man they'd talked about on the news?

I knew one thing for certain, *something* was going on.

20.

The next morning, I woke up to the smell of blueberry pancakes. As soon as that smell registered in my brain, my stomach growled as I sat up in bed and stretched.

I looked over at my alarm clock. It was almost 11 in the morning. After another nice stretch, I hopped out of bed, changed my clothes, and headed downstairs. I felt like I had finally caught up on my sleep.

When I entered the kitchen, I found my parents busily preparing breakfast together.

"Good morning, sleepy head," Mom joked as she mixed the pancake batter.

"Good morning," I said with a smirk. I went to the fridge and poured myself a glass of milk.

"I heard you went on a little adventure last night."

"Yeah, a noise outside woke me up. I thought I saw something when I looked out my window, so I went out to check. I think it was just the wind. It knocked our trash can over."

Mom echoed the warning my dad had given me the night before. The one about getting one of them if it ever happens again. I told her I would.

The smell of the blueberry pancakes was intoxicating. Mom brought over a huge stack and separated them for the three of us. My dad brought a plate of sausage links in one hand, and a bottle of syrup in the other.

He turned the TV onto local news while we ate. During the weekend, local news had time slots every couple of hours in the mornings. At first, they talked about the weather. I didn't care to listen to that, so I stuffed my face with delicious pancakes. It's almost always sunny here in Georgia, anyhow.

Then a news alert broke in.

"More news out of Buford, Georgia this morning," The news lady said. "Police in Buford are on high alert this morning as more reports of the so-called 'Pumpkin Man' have begun to emerge." There was a brief pause as the news channel switched to a police officer interview.

"This again?" my dad asked his mouth full. He sounded slightly concerned.

"We received a few more calls and complaints last night about a man wearing a pumpkin mask. He vandalized a few homes and scared several children. While this appears to be a harmless prank, we are asking parents to be on high alert. We'll patrol the city in full force to ensure this stops," The police officer said. The video cut back to the news anchor.

"And this is exactly why I told you to come get one of us if you see or hear something," my dad said sternly as the news anchor continued.

"Channel 9 News caught up with two teens caught up in the activity last night," The video segued to the teenage boys.

It was Bryce and Tyler! I almost spit my food out.

"We were exploring Echo Park last night, when the Pumpkin Man began chasing after us," Bryce said, his voice shaking.

"It was one of the most terrifying experiences of my life," Tyler added.

The video seemed to skip forward then, because Bryce said, "We didn't get a good look at him. It was dark in the park. Honestly, when he jumped out and screamed at us, we immediately started running for our lives."

The video cut back to the news anchor sitting at her desk.

"There you have it, folks. Please be mindful that while Halloween is a fun holiday, terrorizing children is never okay. Now in sports..."

"Wow! That's so crazy!" Mom said as she finished her plate of food. "I am all for a good scare, but some people take it too far."

"The world is a crazy place," Dad replied.

I helped clean up the dishes, my mind whirling around the news report and the concern spreading across town.

"I mean, I think it's kinda cool," I blurted. Both of my parents turned to look at me.

"What?" my mom asked.

"That someone is taking Halloween seriously and is out scaring people. Halloween is *supposed* to be scary."

"True, but there needs to be limits. Vandalism and tormenting kids in their homes isn't funny,"

"I guess you're right," I said. Before she could say another word, I left the room.

I wanted to get a closer look at Johnny Rotten in the daylight without the wind blowing. Sure enough, I noticed something different about him. His boots appeared to be muddy.

I looked up at Johnny's lollipop eyes expecting him to look back down at me, but he stood as stoic and still as ever before.

"How did you get mud on your boots?" I asked.

My stomach turned in knots. The red paint splotches on our porch step and the muddy boots. It couldn't be...*could it*? I could've asked my parents, but at this point, I think they'd have looked at me like I was crazy.

I turned and headed towards our backyard. My brain was going a mile a minute. Nothing added up. It wasn't even possible! I needed to do something about this and get to the bottom of it.

I decided to try to catch him in the act. If it was him, I was going to find out! The watch I'd gotten for my birthday had an alarm that would vibrate to wake you up. I decided to set it for midnight.

"Johnny Rotten, if you are real, I *will* see for myself tonight," I whispered.

21.

While my parents watched a movie in the living room, I headed up to bed. I knew they wouldn't be up too late as my dad had to work the next day, and my mom had to get up and take me to school.

I laid in bed, reading *Monsters of Mt. Hope* – the third book of the Scareville series, waiting for time to pass. At a little after ten, I began to get sleepy, so I turned the light off and went to sleep.

The next thing I knew, I was jolted awake by my watch. It vibrated on my wrist, and I fumbled around on my bed as I scrambled to turn it off. It was midnight. Time to see if Johnny Rotten was real or not.

I slowly and quietly opened my door. This time, I was extra careful going down the steps, making as little noise as possible.

When I reached the bottom of the stairs, I tiptoed across the living room to our front window. I pulled the blinds open, and to my amazement...I saw Johnny Rotten's head right where it should be. He hadn't moved. He was still here at home.

Disappointed, I closed the blinds and slowly crept back upstairs. Just as I entered my room, I felt something quickly brush across my leg. I looked down, and our cat Smoky let out a horrific screech as he bolted down the stairs.

The sudden high-pitched shriek gave me a mini-heart attack. I did my best to keep myself from screaming and quietly shut my bedroom door.

"Smoky, you're going to be the death of me," I whispered to myself as I got back into bed.

I didn't know whether to feel relieved, or disappointed that Johnny Rotten was still in his spot. Things weren't adding up. How did the red paint splotch on our front step appear? How did he get mud on his boots? What about the rest of the frightening occurrences that I, and other kids in town had experienced?

Finally, even with all these thoughts consuming my mind, I managed to fall back asleep.

22.

The next morning, there were no new reports of the Pumpkin Man. Everything seemed to be business as usual. Dad left for work and, while my mom showered, I ate a bowl of cereal and watched the news.

The whole week went the same way. Nothing out of the ordinary. All the kids and teachers talked about the Pumpkin Man, but there were no new reports.

On Tuesday and Thursday, I tried setting the alarm on my watch to try to catch him. But both times, Johnny Rotten didn't move.

I talked with Ben and Liz about it throughout the week. Both believed Pumpkin Man was some random guy pulling pranks on the town, and he stopped when police started to get serious about it.

I told them how I'd noticed the red splotches of paint on our step, and the mud on Johnny Rotten's boots. They said it was weird, but it just didn't make any sense. Liz told me I was probably letting my imagination get the best of me.

By the time Friday came, the new topic of conversation had turned to the weekend's events. The Buford Halloween Parade was set for Friday night. Every year, Buford ran a huge parade and party in downtown Buford. Businesses would create Halloween-themed floats, and most people in town would watch the parade and collect candy the parade marchers tossed out.

The big news, however, especially in our household, was to take place on Saturday night. That was when the committee came around and selected the best decorated yard in all of Buford. My dad had been talking about it all week long.

"Are you going to come out for the parade?" I asked Ben as we prepared to leave school on Friday afternoon.

"Yeah, I think my parents finally calmed down about the fight. I kept explaining to them that those guys were bullies, and I was just sticking up for you. I think they finally understood and relaxed about it," he replied.

I was happy his parents were no longer mad. I also felt honored that he'd chosen to stand up for me.

"That's great! Maybe our parents can meet up and we can go to the parade together?" I asked hopefully.

"I'll talk to my parents when I get home. I think that would be a lot of fun!" Liz replied.

"Yeah, I'm totally in," Ben said as he headed over toward his bus. "Emily, I'll give you a call after my parents get home from work."

"Okay, sounds good!" I called as Liz and I continued past the buses toward the line where parents picked up their kids.

"I'll call you later and let you know too," Liz said. She gave me a hug and ran over to her dad's car.

"Awesome! Can't wait!" I replied, then hurried over to where my mom waited for me.

I was excited about the parade. The whole town really got into it, and it was a huge weekend for Buford. We were one week away from Halloween, and everything was always so festive. It was my favorite time of the year by far. Between the parade and the decorating contest, there was so much to look forward to. I just hoped we'd beat Sierra and her parents this year.

23.

My parents managed to coordinate with both Ben and Liz's parents, and we met up at a local barbecue restaurant a couple blocks away from the downtown parade.

When we got there, everyone headed to downtown Buford to enjoy the show. All the parents brought chairs, while us kids carried plastic bags to hold the candy in.

We found a good spot to wait for the parade. It was front and center on the sidewalk.

All the businesses and shops downtown closed for the parade. Each had Halloween decorations outside their stores, or Halloween stickers clinging to their windows.

The city workers did a great job. They hung orange pumpkin string lights all over the downtown area, stretching across the main road. They also installed speakers throughout the downtown area. They blared Halloween music while we waited for the event to begin.

Crowds piled in, in droves. The sidewalks on each side began to fill as the sun set. A cool breeze blew through our beautiful downtown.

Excitement filled the air as everyone eagerly waited for the parade to begin. Kids ran around laughing, while the parents sat in their chairs conversing with one another.

Finally, the moment we'd been waiting for arrived. The music stopped, and all the Halloween lights turned off. A roar from the crowd drowned out everything. Suddenly, all the Halloween lights flickered on and off like a strobe light, and what sounded like a loud heartbeat played through the speakers.

The heartbeat grew faster, as did the flickering of the lights. Then, off in the distance, the first parade float slowly made its way down Main Street.

Fireworks went off over downtown from a nearby park, covering Buford in an array of colors and explosions. After the fireworks reached their finale, the crowd went crazy. The lights lining the street went back to normal and Halloween music played through the speakers once more.

By this time, the parade floats were making their way down to us. All the marchers dressed in Halloween costumes tossed candy into the crowd. All of us kids fought to catch them, almost like women trying to catch the bouquet at a wedding.

After a giant dragon float had rolled by, I glanced across the street. To my horror, in an alleyway between two old brick buildings was Johnny Rotten! This time I was sure of it! He was standing there behind the sea of people.

I couldn't see his body, but I knew for sure I'd seen his giant pumpkin head and those lollipop eyes! I grabbed Ben and Liz to show them.

"Ben! Liz!" I called, tugging at their arms and pointing across the road. "Look!"

It was too late. A massive parade float replica of our historic downtown hotel was blocking our view of the other side.

"Yeah, it's a really cool float!" Ben said nonchalantly as he focused on catching candy. Liz completely ignored me as she crouched to grab a piece from the sidewalk.

"No, it was Johnny Rotten! He was across the street!" I cried.

"Emily, stop it. Johnny Rotten isn't real," Liz replied with an eye roll.

"I am telling you guys! He was there in the alleyway right across the street!"

Liz laughed. "Uh-huh. Okay, Emily, nice try."

"I'm not kidding!"

Ben and Liz continued ignoring me and kept catching candy bars.

I was so distraught I didn't even notice the candy bar heading right for me. It bounced off the side of my head and landed with a *thud* on the street.

"Mine!" Ben declared grabbing the candy bar that had just struck my head.

What a jerk.

I couldn't believe my two best friends didn't believe me.

Finally, the float slowly made its way past. I quickly looked back at the place where I'd seen Johnny Rotten. There was no sign of him. My heart sank.

Liz pointed across the street. "See? No one is over there,"

"But he *was* there. I'm telling you!"

Finally, the parade had ended. Our parents seemed in no rush to get back home. They sat in their chairs drinking their beverages. I, however, *wanted* to rush back home. I needed to see if Johnny Rotten was still standing at his post.

"Mom...Dad...come on!" I cried, tugging at their hands.

My father yanked his hand away. "Emily! Settle down!" Go hang out with Ben and Liz. We'll head home in a little bit."

They returned to the conversation they were having with the other adults.

I angrily stomped back over to Ben and Liz. They were seated on the sidewalk, their feet stretched out into the road, digging through their bags of candy.

I took a seat next to them and shot them both an annoyed glance.

"What?" Ben asked, his mouth full of chocolate bar.

"You know what," I replied coldly.

"Oh, come on Emily," Ben said. "You were just trying to scare us."

"Do you really expect us to believe your Halloween prop is somehow alive?" Liz scoffed. She and Ben had a nice chuckle at my expense.

"I know what I saw!" I answered defensively. "Listen, you are my two best friends. I am not trying to scare either of you. I don't know how to explain it, but I'm not making it up."

Ben and Liz looked at each other, then back at me, disbelief still painted on their faces.

"But how though?" Ben asked.

"Look, I don't know. I'm just asking you guys to believe me."

They both sat in silence, each unwrapping another candy bar. Their silence alarmed me. I knew how crazy this must sound, but I knew I was right.

"I guess we'll see if there are any news reports on the Pumpkin Man tomorrow morning. Then we'll know," I declared.

"Okay, so let's say you're right," Liz said. "Let's say Johnny Rotten actually is alive. Then what?"

I didn't have an answer for Liz. I hadn't really thought about it. On one hand, I think it would be cool. On the other hand, what if he was evil?

"I guess I'll figure it out," was all I could muster in response.

Only moments later, our parents came over and told us it was time to go. I didn't get my hopes up about Johnny Rotten being gone when we got home. We'd been away from the house too long.

Sure enough, when we pulled down our road, there he was standing in his normal spot.

I didn't know what to do at this point. My best friends didn't believe me, and my parents would think I was crazy if I tried to discuss it again. I might just have to go on a solo mission to get to the bottom of it.

24.

When we got home, I quickly ran upstairs to my room. I needed to concoct a different plan for tonight. Maybe midnight was too early for me to check and see if Johnny Rotten was still in his spot.

I needed some sort of proof though. I didn't want to be ignored anymore. I snuck across the hall to my parents' bedroom and grabbed my dad's camera. I brought it back to my room and put it in my dresser drawer. Then, I changed into my pajamas and flopped on my bed.

I set my watch alarm for two a.m. and stared at the drawing of Johnny Rotten hanging on my wall. I couldn't wrap my mind around how any of this could be remotely possible. I just wanted to confirm I wasn't crazy.

I really hoped my plan would work.

My parents came up and said goodnight a little while later.

"Tomorrow's the big day!" my dad exclaimed. He smiled as he shut my bedroom door.

He was right about that. I was excited for tomorrow, but right now, my focus was on proving that my creation—my Spirit of Halloween—was indeed alive.

Mere moments seemed to pass after I shut my eyes. Soon, my watch aggressively buzzed on my wrist and woke me up. I gasped in fright as I sat up in bed, collected my thoughts for a moment, then grabbed my dad's camera. I snuck downstairs.

My heart pounded as I inched closer to the front window of our house. My palms began to sweat and my breathing grew shallow and loud. One more step to the window.

I tugged the curtains open.

If it were possible for my eyes to bulge out of my head, it would have happened.

Johnny Rotten was nowhere to be found.

I scampered to our front door, unlocked it and opened it as quietly as I could. Then, I stepped out onto our porch and shut the door behind me.

I turned to Johnny Rotten's spot. He wasn't there!

I'd thought this would be an exciting moment, but truth be told, I have never been so scared in my entire life.

I hurried down the front steps and made my way through the dewy grass. The only thing remaining in his spot was a couple of imprints from his big boots.

My heart seemed to jump out of my chest and into my throat. My mouth was dry, and my stomach was in absolute knots.

I had hoped for this moment, but deep down, I never *actually* thought it would happen. No matter what my brain told me.

I took a couple of steps back and snapped a photo of the spot where our missing Halloween prop had been.

As I took the photo, leaves rustled, and twigs snapped. The sound came from the strip of shrubs and trees separating our house from that of our neighbors.

I froze. What if it was Johnny Rotten? What was I going to do?

A shiver ran up my spine as the noises fell silent. I wanted to turn and look, but I couldn't.

Then, the sounds started again. I forced myself to turn and see what was making the ruckus this time.

Whatever it was, it was beyond the reach of our Halloween lighting. I could barely make out the movement of the branches and bushes. My breathing became shallower and much more rapid. I felt sick to my stomach, standing all alone in our front yard absolutely trembling with fear.

Suddenly, a deer emerged from the tree line. It galloped across the yard and out of sight.

A sense of relief came over me and I realized something. I had to show my mom and dad!

I didn't even care about being noisy this time as I ran back inside the house. I rushed up the stairs and knocked on their bedroom door.

"Mom...Dad! I have to show you something!" I yelled.

Something shuffled in the bedroom, followed by footsteps as my dad opened the bedroom door.

"Emily, do you realize what time it is? What's wrong?" he asked as I ducked under his arm and entered their bedroom.

"Johnny Rotten is gone," I said as I took a seat at the foot of their bed.

"Gone? What do you mean gone?"

"He's real Dad! I told you he was real! He isn't in his spot, he's gone!"

"What? That's impossible, honey." He left the bedroom and hurried downstairs.

I followed with my mom trailing close behind at my heels, as we made our way to our front door. Dad opened the door, and I waited for him to say I was right.

Dad waved an arm out toward the front yard. "You, see? He's right where he always is. You were having a bad dream."

"Huh?"

I peeked out the door and, sure enough, Johnny Rotten was standing right where he always stood. I couldn't believe it.

"Dad, it wasn't a dream! I used your camera and took a photo for proof!" I pleaded as he closed the front door and locked it.

"Wait...you took my camera?"

"Yes, but that's not important. I have photo proof to show he was gone just minutes ago!

I flipped open the screen and clicked on the menu to show him the photo.

My heart sank. The only photo on the camera was a giant white flash. You couldn't see anything.

"B-but..." I stammered.

"But nothing, young lady. You are going to march upstairs, and we are going to talk about this tomorrow," Dad scolded.

He snatched his camera away from me before I went upstairs. I felt like crying. I had proof, and just like that, everything had fallen apart.

25.

The next morning was a tumultuous one. Mom and Dad woke me up at the crack of dawn and made me dust all the furniture, vacuum, and mop all the floors while they sat in the living room and watched TV. I had almost finished mopping the tile floor in the kitchen when a news break came on the TV.

It was another breaking story out of Buford involving the Pumpkin Man. Reports had come in stating that Pumpkin Man had been out around town scaring kids and vandalizing yards once again.

When I heard the news anchor say, "And our very own Billy Batcher is on the scene," I put my mop away.

"Hey, that's the Blankenships' yard," Dad said from the living room.

I hurried over to join my parents and see what was going on.

Billy Batcher was interviewing Mr. Blankenship on the TV.

"Whoever did this is an absolute monster," I heard Mr. Blankenship say before the camera switched to their yard. All of their Halloween decorations and props were covered in bubblegum-pink paint.

"Whoa!" I cried.

I ran over to our front window and looked out. Sure enough, the big news van and camera crew were across the street talking to Mr. Blankenship.

Mom and Dad joined me and peered out the window as well. Mom gasped.

It was bad. You could see it all the way across the street. All their decorations were ruined.

"Who would do such a thing?" Mom asked.

Neither Dad nor I answered.

After all the excitement of the morning, we finally sat down and had breakfast. Afterward, I headed upstairs and immediately called Ben and Liz, using the video chat on my tablet.

They'd seen the news and couldn't believe someone would do such a thing. I asked them to come over. They both said they would.

After the call, I thought back to when I'd drawn Johnny Rotten. I know I'd said I wished he were real. I'd wanted him to make Halloween scary again and punish those who didn't respect the holiday, but I never in a thousand years would have thought he could *actually* do it.

26.

When I came downstairs, I heard yelling coming from our front yard. I went outside to see what was going on. My dad and Mr. Blankenship were standing at the end of our driveway in the middle of an argument. I took a seat in the rocking chair on our front porch and watched. I didn't want to get in the middle of it.

"I know you did it, Riggs! Who else would do something like this? You were just afraid of losing again this year!" Mr. Blankenship shouted.

"I have no clue what you're talking about," Dad said. "I would never do something like that. This competition has always been a friendly rivalry."

The argument continued and ended with Mr. Blankenship flailing his arms wildly. He yelled several words I'm not allowed to say, before storming back over to his yard.

Dad approached our front steps and threw his arms in the air.

"Can you believe that guy?" he asked, as he stomped into the house. He didn't wait for my reply. He just slammed the door.

What a mess this had turned into. I gazed at the back of Johnny Rotten's big pumpkin head.

I regretted ever drawing him.

Finally, Ben and Liz rode over on their bikes. They parked them in our driveway. I walked out to meet them.

"Man, the Blankenships yard is trashed!" Ben said with a laugh.

"It's not funny, Ben," I replied. "Mr. Blankenship thinks my dad did it."

"Why would he think tha-...Oh! Yeah. The rivalry."

"So, you really think this thing is alive?" Liz asked, quivering, as we approached Johnny Rotten.

"Yes, I know it for a fact now. I confirmed it last night before things fell apart. He *IS* the Pumpkin Man from the news," I replied, staring up at Johnny Rotten's face.

"I gotta see it," Ben said. He kicked Johnny's boot.

Ben's words gave me my lightbulb moment. I had an idea.

"In the off-chance Johnny Rotten can hear us, I want to head out back to discuss the plan," I said. Ben and Liz agreed.

When we got to the back patio, we took seats around the table, and I laid out my plan. I was going to get permission to stay the night with Liz. We would sneak out together and meet Ben by my house around midnight.

"I'm just supposed to sneak out in the middle of the night by myself?" he asked. "What about curfew? What if I get caught?"

"Look, you said you wanted to see Johnny Rotten moving around, this is how we have to do it," I said.

The plan was set. I asked my parents for permission to stay the night at Liz's house. My dad was a little upset I wasn't going to be around when the judges came to critique our decorations, though.

"They won't announce the winners until Sunday morning on the news anyhow," I said.

"That's true."

When I walked Ben and Liz back to their bikes, we found Sierra and Kelly waiting at the end of the driveway. Sierra had a scowl on her face that would scare away even the fiercest monster. She looked red and angry.

"How dare you and your dad destroy our decorations," Sierra said, as she and Kelly marched forward.

"Look. We didn't mess with your yard," I replied. I didn't have the patience to deal with Sierra's drama today.

"Oh, I suppose the Pumpkin Man did it?" Kelly said sarcastically.

"I don't know...I guess? I just know it wasn't us. We wouldn't have needed to this year. Our yard was *way* better than yours."

"I guess we'll never know," Sierra said. She sounded absolutely shaken. "You better watch your back. I'll be watching you."

She and Kelly stormed off.

"What is that supposed to mean?" I asked Ben and Liz.

My friends shrugged. They hopped on their bikes and rode off.

In a way, I felt bad for Sierra, but at the same time, I didn't. She'd been bullying me for years. Sometimes karma really does come for those who deserve it. Anyhow, I had bigger fish to fry tonight.

27.

After my dad dropped me off at Liz's house, we ate dinner and went upstairs to her bedroom to get ready for the night.

Liz's bedroom was similar to mine. She had posters of her celebrity crushes, as well as Halloween stuff taped to her walls. She had a similar dresser to mine. The only real differences in our rooms were that she had a TV and two nightstands, one on either side of the bed, instead of having just one like me. A small fishbowl, with a single goldfish in it, stood on one night stand, while a lamp sat on the other.

Liz turned on her TV and switched it to a Halloween movie.

"What do you think is going to happen?" Liz, she asked, as the film began.

"I'm not sure," I replied. "I just want people to believe that this isn't some random guy in a costume doing all this stuff."

"What do you think it wants?"

"Honestly, if it turns out Johnny Rotten is alive, and it's based on my creation and how I envisioned things when I drew him, then he wants to make Halloween scary again. He wants to punish those who don't treat the holiday with the respect it deserves."

"What a crazy world we live in," Liz responded. We both laughed.

Time seemed to move at a snail's pace. Mostly because we both couldn't wait to see Johnny Rotten with our own two eyes. Even though I'd seen him missing, I'd never actually *seen* him running around.

Finally, the clock struck midnight. Liz and I shared an anxious glance as we snuck out of her room. All the lights were off and, thankfully, both her parents were in bed.

Liz had grabbed a small flashlight from her parents' junk drawer in the kitchen when they weren't looking, and now, she clicked it on. We crept down the staircase and out her front door.

The night air had a very cool, crisp, fall feel to it on this night as we walked across the street. A thin layer of fog had rolled in, and the wet grass felt squishy as we sloshed through Liz's neighbor's yards towards my house.

Unfortunately, we had to cut through the Blankenships' yard. I just hoped they were sleeping already.

As we drew nearer to my house, the fog seemed to grow thicker and thicker. An ominous and foreboding vibe pierced through the night air and directly into our souls.

We made our way through the Blankenships' backyard and headed toward the front corner of their house. We peeked around it and, just as sure as the sun would rise, there was Johnny Rotten perched in his normal spot.

While we hunkered down in our hiding spot, Ben wandered aimlessly down the sidewalk toward our house. He seemed scared to be walking around by himself.

"Psst! Ben!" I whispered loudly. Ben stopped dead in his tracks.

"Ben! Over here!" Liz whispered a little louder. She pointed her flashlight in his direction.

Ben noticed the light and came running over.

"Sheesh. You guys scared me," he whispered.

"Sorry, we weren't trying to scare you. We just wanted you to know where we were," I replied. The three of us turned to Johnny Rotten, who remained firmly planted in his spot.

The silence was deafening. There wasn't a soul outside except for us. The fog that blanketed the neighborhood seemed to grow thicker and thicker with each minute that flew by.

"So, when's this thing gonna move?" Ben asked.

"If I knew that answer, I would already have surefire proof to show you guys," I countered.

The waiting game was on. Time seemed to move at a standstill as we cowered by the corner of the Blankenship home. Everything was still.

Suddenly, a voice rang out from behind us.

"What are you guys doing here?"

It was Sierra!

We turned to see her and Kelly standing behind us with their arms folded, and evil scowls contorting their faces.

"I knew you were behind ruining our Halloween decorations!" Sierra said coldly. "I should go wake my dad right now and tell him what's going on."

Sierra and Kelly turned toward the back of the house. I couldn't let them wake her dad.

"Don't wake him up! Look, it wasn't us. It was Johnny Rotten," I cried.

Both Kelly and Sierra came to a screeching halt and turned back to look at us.

"Who's Johnny Rotten?" Sierra asked.

"It's what I named my drawing. The one we based our main Halloween decoration on," I replied

"That ugly thing?" Sierra said. "Wait...where is it?"

28.

"Huh?" Liz, Ben, and I said in unison as we spun around.

To our shock and awe, Johnny Rotten was gone. Nowhere to be seen. My heart began to pound, and it became harder to breathe.

"It...It can't be," Ben sputtered, his jaw dropping, eyes wide.

"What is this? Some kinda sick joke?" Kelly demanded.

"I wish I could say it was," I answered. "He was literally there just a minute ago."

"There's no way," Sierra said. "Do you really think we're dumb enough to fall for one of your stupid pranks?"

"Listen, believe us or don't. We're going to try to solve this. You can come with us or stay here by yourselves," I replied. There was no sense in continuing this argument.

"Fine. We'll come along. But if there's any funny business, we'll head back here and tell my dad you guys were responsible for everything," Sierra replied. She nodded to her friend Kelly.

Now our trio had become a five-person team. All of us were in a search for an answer as we trekked through the dense fog and down the sidewalk.

"Where do you suppose it went?" Liz asked with wide eyes and a shaky voice.

"Probably under your bed...ooh spooky," Sierra joked, as she and Kelly cracked themselves up.

The laughter was short-lived, however. We all froze dead in our tracks when a tree branch snap in the wooded area right next to us.

"What was that?" Kelly hissed.

"This isn't funny guys," Sierra added.

"It wasn't us, now shut up!" I whispered, squinting into the dark wooded area.

Nothing was moving and things fell silent once more. My heart raced, and everyone's breathing grew louder.

Suddenly, I came to the realization that it wasn't us breathing that loudly. Someone was breathing *very* heavily behind us!

The others must've realized the same thing, because all five of us turned at the same exact time. To our horror, there stood Johnny Rotten!

A mix of screams and yelling filled the air as we panicked. The tall figure towered over us, grinning from ear to ear as he bellowed out a deep, monstrous laugh.

None of us moved. We were all paralyzed with fear. All we could do was stare in frightened disbelief.

"Happy Halloween!" cried Johnny Rotten. He made a strange gurgling noise...and then...

"BLEEHHH!" he proceeded to vomit pumpkin guts all over the five of us. We erupted into a sea of screams.

"Run!" Ben yelled. We all turned, trying to escape.

Before I could get very far, I felt something wrap around my ankle and yank hard. I tripped and fell with a hard *thump* onto the road. Johnny Rotten had grabbed hold of my ankle and was now standing right over top of me.

"Guys! Help!" I screamed at the top of my lungs.

"You gave me life once again. You and I will be together forever. You are mine!" Johnny Rotten hissed in his deep, monstrous voice. He bent down and grabbed my shoulders with both of his wet, leafy hands.

I struggled and yelled for help. I was absolutely horrified. What did he mean, "We will be together forever"?

Out of nowhere, Ben and Liz came crashing into Johnny Rotten, knocking him off me.

"Come on Emily! Hurry!" Ben, lifted me to my feet and we ran as fast and hard as our bodies would allow.

When I turned to look back, Johnny Rotten had vanished.

"Where are Sierra and Kelly?" I asked. We continued running as fast as we could, all while trying to scrape the pumpkin guts off ourselves.

"I think they managed to get back to Sierra's house already," Liz answered.

"Guys, I don't want to run all the way back to my house alone!" Ben said. We slowed down to a brisk walk trying to catch our breath.

Liz and I agreed to take Ben back to his house before we went back to Liz's.

We wound up cutting through a bunch of yards before making it to Ben's house. There, he promptly scraped off the remaining pumpkin guts and went inside.

"Thanks for coming. Be careful," he said, as he shut the door and turned the lock.

"Great, now we have the long road to get back to my house," Liz said.

"Let's just get there in one piece," I said as I finished scraping all the pumpkin guts off. "So gross."

"Alright, let's go," Liz said.

We started jogging through the neighboring yards.

I was shocked that we made it back to Liz's house without running into Johnny Rotten. I didn't let Liz catch on, but I was deathly afraid he would catch us and take me away.

We rushed up to her front door and then turned to look back. Johnny Rotten was standing across the road, staring straight at us. Liz hurried us inside, shut the door and locked it.

"Should we wake my mom and dad?" Liz asked.

"And do what? Tell them my Halloween decoration is trying to kill us?" I replied. "No way!"

We made our way over to Liz's front window. Johnny Rotten was gone. Vanished in a matter of seconds once again.

"I still don't get how any of this is possible," Liz said.

"Me neither, but we're going to find out," I replied. We snuck upstairs and into her room.

We had a difficult time falling asleep. Then again, how do you fall asleep after a traumatizing experience like that?

29.

When Liz and I woke up the next morning, everything felt like a bad dream. My body ached, and my knee had been scraped when Johnny Rotten tripped me.

Neither of us could accurately portray the kind of fear we experienced as we reflected on last night's events.

"I think I know the answer to your question now," I told Liz.

"What question?" she asked.

"About what Johnny Rotten wants. He wants me," I said with a shudder. "He told me last night that we would be together forever, and that I was his."

"I won't let it get you. He can't move around in the daytime. What's stopping us from just burning him to the ground?"

"Are you kidding?" I scoffed. "My parents would kill me. They worked so hard making him."

The sun breathed warm life into the room as we brainstormed in silence.

"We just need to figure out how to stop him from coming to life somehow," I blurted.

Before either of us could say anything, Liz's mom came up and knocked on the door. She said Ben was on the phone asking for us.

We quickly rushed downstairs and told Ben our problem. He asked us to come over to his house so we could figure it out together.

Liz and I quickly changed out of our pajamas and into our regular clothes. We told her parents we were going to visit Ben and would be back later.

Ben greeted us at the front door and welcomed us into his home. He had bags under his eyes, and his hair looked disheveled. It looked like he hadn't slept much either.

He led us over to his family's office where they all shared a computer.

"I know you had mentioned finding a way to stop Johnny Rotten," Ben said. "And it got me thinking, what is Johnny Rotten?"

Ben plopped down in the computer chair and pulled up a search engine. Liz and I stood on either side of him.

"I mean...he was my creation," I answered. I was confused as to where Ben was going with this.

"Right, right. It needs to be more than that though," Ben said. He waved his hands, as though trying to get me to elaborate. "What went into the creation process?"

"Well, when we got back from looking at all the Halloween decorations, I began to miss the old days of Halloween, when things were scary.

"I went home and wished Halloween was scary again. I daydreamed about what I thought the Spirit of Halloween might look like. Then, I drew it and wished it would come to life. I wanted it to scare the people who didn't respect the holiday."

"That's it!" Ben cried. He began typing into the search bar.

"What's *it*?" Liz asked.

"We were looking at this the wrong way the whole time. We viewed Johnny Rotten as this horrible monster, when in all actuality, it's a spirit using Johnny Rotten's form to do its bidding," Ben said this as if it were a simple math equation.

"Look. See for yourself."

Ben had typed into the search bar, *creating a spirit with your imagination*. All sorts of articles and blogs popped up. Most of them were about this thing called a *tulpa*.

Tulpas were spirits who could come to life through the imagination of a creator. Tulpas gained more strength and power as people heard about them and spread stories about them.

That actually made sense. The news coverage of The Pumpkin Man must have given him more power.

"Do any of these articles say how to stop it?" I asked.

Ben clicked on another article. "It says here you need to sever your connection to it."

We paused and looked at one another.

"You have to destroy your drawing!" Liz exclaimed.

"That's it!" I replied. "But what if it doesn't work?"

"It'll work if you believe it will," Ben replied. "You have to believe, Emily."

"Okay it'll work," I said.

Liz and I decided to leave Ben's. We apologized for the short trip, but we wanted to destroy the picture before anyone got hurt.

We had to go to my house and go now.

We made our way through the neighborhood to my house, swinging around the front to confirm Johnny Rotten was back in his normal resting spot. Ironically enough, I noticed a single strand of dried-up pumpkin gut, with one pumpkin seed, dangling from the corner of his mouth.

"So disgusting," Liz commented. She poked at the seed.

"Right," I replied. I was just thankful that he hadn't disappeared.

"Hey, Emily!" I heard Sierra yell from across the street.

Liz and I turned, as she marched toward us.

"Look...I just wanted to say I'm sorry," she said.

"Sorry for what?" I asked.

"I'm sorry for being so mean to you guys," she answered, timidly, "and I am sorry for accusing you of destroying our Halloween decorations.

"It's okay. And thank you."

"So…What are we going to do about this guy?" she nodded in the direction of Johnny Rotten.

We filled Sierra in on the research we'd done, and explained how we were going to take care of it.

She seemed relieved we'd found an answer, and that we were ending the nightmare that was Johnny Rotten.

Liz and I hurried into the house. Before we could make our way upstairs, my dad came over and gave me a giant hug.

"We won the decorating contest!" Dad said. "It turns out the committee really *loved* Johnny Rotten."

Liz and I giggled nervously.

"That's great Dad!" I said, as Liz and I raced upstairs to my room.

Once inside, we took the picture out of its frame. I tore the drawing in half and tossed it into the trashcan next to my bed.

"There we go. No more Johnny Rotten," I said, wiping my hands emphatically.

"Thank goodness," Liz grinned.

30.

All had gone off without a hitch. Everything seemed to be back to business as usual. A couple of days had passed since I tore my drawing in half, and there had been no more reports of Pumpkin Man on the news. Even the vandalism and fright that had befallen Buford had finally been silenced.

I felt like the weight of the world had been lifted off my shoulders. My friends and I could finally get back to living our normal lives without being terrorized.

We were just days away from Halloween, and the whole town was buzzing once again. On my way home from school, everyone on the school bus chattered about being ready for trick or treat and which candy they were most excited for. My personal favorite was the pumpkin shaped Reese's cups. I mean, chocolate and peanut butter, what could go wrong?

The school bus dropped me off at home and, as I made my way up the driveway, I sneered at Johnny Rotten and stuck my tongue out. I was so relieved he could no longer come to life.

Neither of my parents were home. Normally, my dad tried to be home when I got back from school. Maybe, he'd run into town for something really quick. I shrugged it off as I marched up the front porch steps and entered our house.

I tossed my backpack to the floor, and it fell with a *thud*. I plopped down on our comfy couch and sighed.

In the kitchen, Smoky munched away on his kibble. That reminded me I too was hungry. My stomach growled in disapproval.

I hopped up and rushed into the kitchen to grab a snack. Smoky glanced up indifferently before going back to his food.

I really wanted to tear into the Halloween candy early but thought better of it. A cookie would have to hold me over until dinner. I reached into our snack cabinet and noticed a note on the kitchen counter, a $20 bill underneath. The note from my dad said:

-Emily-

Had to run into town to meet your mother at the Museum for their Halloween art event. We will be home around 9-ish. Feel free to order food. If you have any issues, please reach out to the Blankenships.

Oh! By the way, I was taking the trash out this morning and noticed your drawing had been torn in two. You will be happy to know that I fixed it and got it taped back together. I brought it with me. Going to display it at tonight's event.

Sorry I forgot to mention this beforehand, I completely forgot.

Love,

Dad

My heart sank. I couldn't believe what I was seeing. I actually had to do a double-take and read the note twice.

I even pinched myself to make sure this wasn't some messed-up dream. Sure enough, this wasn't a dream.

"Oh, no..." I whispered in disbelief.

I sprang into action and ran over to our house phone. I often gave my parents a hard time about still having one of these things, but boy was I glad we had one now.

I frantically punched in the numbers and called Ben first, and then Liz to give them the horrific news. They both agreed to meet up in front of my house as soon as possible.

I was in absolute tunnel vision. I hurried out the front door and locked it behind me as my heart continued to beat at a frenetic pace. *What were we going to do?*

31.

I stood out on our front porch, waiting on Ben and Liz as I glared at the back of Johnny Rotten's enormous head. I don't know how long I'd been staring at him, but I was snapped back to reality when I heard Sierra call out from across the street.

"Hey, Emily!" she yelled.

Sierra sprinted across the street toward my house. I know we had recently re-kindled our friendship, but I was still shocked to see her coming up my driveway to greet me.

Sierra shot me a disgruntled look as she mounted our porch steps.

"Hey to you too," she said coldly.

"Huh? What? Sorry," I replied.

"What's wrong?"

"The drawing..."

"What about it?"

I was just about to answer when Ben and Liz came into sight, pedaling their bikes furiously down the road. They came to a screeching halt in my driveway and tossed their bikes aside. They rushed up to us and Sierra shot me a concerned glance.

"What's going on?" she asked.

"My dad fixed the picture of Johnny Rotten," I told her, my voice filled with dread.

"He what?" Sierra exclaimed. "Why didn't you flush it down the toilet or something?"

"I-I didn't think he would notice, or care enough to fix it," I replied. Ben and Liz ran up then and gave me a hug.

"Why don't you just destroy it now?" Sierra cried.

"Because it isn't here. He took it to the museum where my mom works for some Halloween event they're having tonight."

"So, what's the plan?" Ben asked.

"We have to get it back before the sun sets," I said.

"And how are we going to do that?" Liz questioned.

"We're going to go to the museum and destroy it once and for all." I was bound and determined not to let Johnny Rotten gain power again at nightfall.

We gathered up our bikes. To my surprise, Sierra said she was going to tag along and help.

This was it. This was our moment. We needed to make sure Johnny Rotten would stay put.

We pedaled our hearts out trying to get to the museum as quickly as possible. The parking lot was jam packed.

"Man, this is crazy!" Ben exclaimed as we placed our bikes in the rack and locked them in place.

The sun was beginning to set as we marched up to the front of the museum. A security guard greeted us at the steps.

The husky man held his arms up like a shield, preventing us from going in. "Hey, where do you kids think you are going? Can't you read the sign?" He motioned toward a sign which read:

Adult beverages served – No one under 21 permitted.

"But my drawing is inside there!" I protested.

"I understand that, but I'm sorry. No children allowed," He ushered us away from the front of the building.

"Great! What are we going to do now?" I cried out as we made our way back over toward our bikes.

An eerie silence fell over our group. We all seemed to be in the same boat. There was nothing we *could* do at this point.

The sun seemed to be setting at a much faster rate than before. A mix of grey and orange light painted downtown Buford as it dimmed.

"Maybe we can try to sneak in?" Ben suggested.

"Ha! And then what? My parents know what all of us look like," I said, shaking my head in frustration.

Stunned silence fell over the four of us once again as night crept up on us.

"Well, we can't just sit here and wait around," Liz urged. "We need to do something."

"And what are you proposing we do?" Sierra asked.

"Call the police?"

"No...No that won't work," I said. "We need to get back to the house before he harms anyone else."

"And then what?" Sierra asked.

"I'm not sure. We'll figure it out when we get there." We unlocked our bikes from the rack.

The ride back toward my house was an ominous one. A sense of foreboding and apprehension filled my mind as we cautiously rode through the heart of Buford.

Darkness had fallen when we reached the outskirts of downtown. A heavy breeze whipped through the night sky, sending a chill down my spine.

As we were passing by an old, abandoned factory, we all heard a loud *crash.* It came from the decrepit building and sounded like metal being thrown around. We slammed on our brakes and stopped. My heart began beating out of my chest.

"What was that?" Liz hissed.

We rode our bikes closer to the factory, hoping to discover the source of the noise we'd heard.

"Please be a raccoon. Please be a raccoon," I whispered while my stomach did somersaults.

A heavy silence fell over us. Suddenly, heavy bootsteps rushed through the asphalt parking lot, followed by the rustling of overgrown brush maybe thirty feet away.

"Let's get out of here!" Sierra screamed.

Without warning, like a bolt of lightning, Johnny Rotten came darting out of the nearby brush. He crashed into Ben and his bike, sending both toppling over with a hard *thud*.

Before any of us could react, Johnny Rotten grabbed Ben by his ankles, and like a slingshot, pulled him away from us. He ran toward the dark factory and out of sight, with Ben screaming at the top of his lungs.

"Ben!" I screamed as I leaped off my bike and began to chase after him. My bike fell to the pavement, but I didn't care.

Sierra and Liz bickered with each other for a moment, and then their bikes fell to the ground as well.

I heard the snapping of branches and rustling of grass away off in the distance. Ben's screams were growing faint. I continued to scream out after him, running as fast as my legs would allow.

I was operating off pure adrenaline at this point. Nothing else mattered except saving Ben.

In the distance, I heard the horrifying and boisterous laughter of Johnny Rotten.

"Emily! Emily! Wait up!" I heard Liz yell from behind me.

I slowed and turned just as they caught up to me. All of us were out of breath.

"Come on! We don't have any time to waste! We need to go save Ben!" I demanded.

"But what if it is a trap?" Sierra asked.

"If that were you in there, would you want us to leave you behind?" I spat back at her.

"No." Sierra pulled her phone out of her pocket and turned on her flashlight. "I guess we might need this."

I had always resented Sierra for having a smartphone when I wasn't allowed to have one, but in this instance, I was super relieved she had it.

We were making our way toward the side of the factory building, when we heard another *loud* crash, almost like a door slamming shut. Then, everything fell silent again.

"He took Ben inside!" I yelled as we raced toward the side entrance of the factory.

Deep in the depths of my soul, I knew we shouldn't be entering the factory. I knew it wasn't safe, but still, the only thing on my mind was getting Ben back safely.

The side entrance was an old rusty door with a cracked, glass window at the top of it. I yanked at the door, but it wouldn't budge. I called for Sierra and Liz to help me. Now my biggest fear was that Ben was locked inside the creepy factory with Johnny Rotten.

The three of us tugged and tugged with all our might. Finally, the heavy door swung open and sent the three of us toppling backward. We hit the pavement, one on top of the other.

We got back on our feet and cautiously made our way inside the abandoned building.

The foul smell of mold in the long-forgotten paper mill filled our nostrils. Even with the flashlight from Sierra's phone, visibility was difficult in the vast building. Debris was scattered over the floor, and in the distance, we could make out the outlines of the giant machines used to print materials.

My heart had to be going a mile a minute. I felt sick, as though I needed to throw up. Inside the building, everything was still and silent. The place would be frightening enough in its own right, even if we weren't chasing an evil monster around.

"Ben!" I whispered hoarsely. "Ben!"

"Why are you whispering?" Sierra asked. "It's not like Johnny Rotten doesn't know we're in here. That door was too loud."

She had a point. I shouted for Ben as we moved into the depths of the factory, navigating around all the dangerous and rusty machinery.

When we heard a loud shuffling of paper off in the distance, followed by an ear-piercing scream from Ben, we all froze.

Safety was of no concern to me anymore. I darted off toward the source of the sound, bobbing and weaving through the maze of machines.

"Emily! Wait for us!" Liz yelled.

At this point, I didn't have time to waste.

"Ben!" I called out as loud as I could.

More rustling, followed by another scream from Ben. I was getting closer.

I ran around a giant cylindrical press and came to a screeching halt when I reached the other side.

There, towering over me, stood the outline of Johnny Rotten.

Liz and Sierra trailed off way behind me. Occasionally Sierra's light shone in my general direction, illuminating Johnny Rotten's gruesome face and the nearby surroundings.

I stood completely still, paralyzed with fear, while Ben writhed around and struggled in Johnny Rotten's grip. He clutched at Ben as though he were a hostage.

"Let him go!" I demanded through gritted teeth.

The horrifying brute didn't speak. He merely let out a deep and troubling snicker.

"I said let him go!"

"Oh, but where's the fun in that?" he taunted in his harsh, growl of a voice. "Did you think it would be that easy to get rid of me?"

Ben let out a grunt of pain.

"Just let him go! It's not him you want," I replied, ignoring his question. "You want me. Let him go and take me!"

"Emily, no!" Ben croaked.

"Very well," Johnny grumbled, tossing Ben aside like a rag doll. He sent him crashing into one of the nearby machines. Ben fell to the floor and lay there, motionless.

"Ben!" I screamed.

Before I could run toward him and make sure he was okay, Johnny Rotten grabbed hold of me and attempted to drag me off, just as Sierra and Liz rounded the corner.

"Let Emily go!" Liz cried.

Johnny Rotten let out a hiss, "No! She is mine!"

I struggled against Johnny's grip, but he was too strong. His long wispy fingers wrapped around me like ropes, while his powerful arms kept me pinned close to him.

"She is not yours! Let her go!" Liz yelled again.

"Yeah, let her go you big, ugly oaf!" Sierra added.

"She *is* mine. She gave me life. We will be together forever!" he growled, his grip tightening. I could hardly breathe.

Next to us, Ben stirred. He groaned as Liz and Sierra rushed over to help him up.

"Emily!" he cried, wincing with pain.

In the light from Sierra's phone, I saw a stream of blood ooze from his forehead.

I couldn't find the words to call back to him. Fear was taking over. My whole body felt like it was about to shut down, even though my heart felt like it was beating out of my chest.

"It was never about the drawing Emily!" he grunted.

"What?" Liz and Sierra said.

"Think about it!" Ben croaked once again, still in pain. "The drawing was just a product of your imagination. Nothing more than a symbol of what your mind created..."

"Hush boy!" Johnny snarled.

"You have to convince yourself he isn't real, Emily! You have to convince yourself that he isn't alive!"

"I said hush, boy!"

Ben was right. Even through all this fear, I had to convince myself that Johnny Rotten wasn't real, that he could no longer come to life. I had to cast him out of my brain and see him as nothing more than a Halloween prop.

I closed my eyes and cleared my mind. I thought back to all the fun times my family and I had at Halloween. Before Johnny Rotten. I imagined Johnny Rotten as something adored by many in the community, but nothing more than a prop we stored away in the basement for the rest of the year.

"You aren't real!" I croaked, still struggling for air.

"You aren't real!" Johnny Rotten mimicked. Taunting me and Ben. His deep, demonic voice was enough to make your skin crawl, but I couldn't focus on that.

"Keep going, Emily!" Ben said as Johnny Rotten continued to cackle and shoot barbs at all of us.

I closed my eyes tighter this time. I kept telling myself he wasn't real. I thought about the future. About next Halloween and how we had to drag Johnny Rotten out of our basement. He was just a prop.

"You aren't real!" I choked out again.

Johnny's grip loosened. Ben, Liz, and Sierra cheered me on and told me to keep going.

"I am in control here! You came from my brain! You are nothing more than a Halloween prop!"

Just like that, like the push of a button, Johnny Rotten released me.

I backpedaled away from Johnny Rotten as he began to make weird gurgling noises and his body spasmed and shook wildly.

"No!" he screamed as he staggered toward the four of us.

In unison, all four of us yelled, "You aren't real!"

He stopped dead in his tracks and shook even more violently. Strange noises emanated from deep inside him. He let out an earth-shattering roar, that sent a jolt of fear through my entire body.

Johnny Rotten took another slow step toward us. Then another, almost as if he was walking through wet cement. Still convulsing and making weird gurgling noises he took another step.

Suddenly, he stopped right in front of us. There was a moment where it felt like everything stood still, and then...

"BLEEHHH!"

Again, Johnny Rotten vomited pumpkin guts all over the four of us. It seemed like a never-ending supply. We were completely covered in the sticky goop as pumpkin seeds bounced around the factory floor.

We stood completely still, exchanging glances with one another. The four of us were frozen in place. What just happened? Had we won? We were all absolutely stunned and terrified. Johnny Rotten stood still like a statue as well. Things in the factory fell silent. You could've heard a pin drop.

"Ugh. So disgusting. Not this again," Ben joked, wiping himself off.

None of us could help ourselves. We all laughed.

"I-I think it worked!" I exclaimed, brushing myself off as well.

"Thank god!" Sierra replied. She pointed her flashlight up at Johnny Rotten one more time, just to be sure.

He stood as still as the day he was made.

I turned to Ben and made sure he was okay. He was a trooper for sure.

"Thank you, Ben," I said. "Thank you for helping me see past the fear. It feels like the world has been lifted off my shoulders."

We all joined together in a giant group hug.

"So, uh guys..." Liz said. "How are we getting Johnny Rotten back to the house?"

We all groaned as we realized we'd have to drag this heavy, horrifying Halloween prop back to my house.

Sierra glanced down at her phone. "It's 8:24," she said.

I sighed. We were going to have to hurry if we wanted to get Johnny back to the house. After that, we'd have to return and get our bikes before my parents got home.

35.

Somehow, we managed. The occasional car passed by and honked at us as we carried the big galoot back home, but we made it.

Once we got back to our bikes, the four of us shared one more hug before going our separate ways.

Just as I parked my bike in the garage, my parents pulled up the driveway.

I sprinted toward them and gave each a giant hug as they got out of the car. They both seemed a bit taken aback by the gesture, but happy to receive it.

"Well, how was your night kiddo?" Mom asked as we walked into the house.

I let out an exasperated sigh, "Oh, nothing out of the ordinary. You know, normal day."

I couldn't tell them the truth about what happened. They'd throw me in the looney bin. I was just so thankful to be at home and safe with them, knowing Johnny Rotten would never be an issue again.

"Were you out smashing pumpkins tonight?" My dad asked.

"Huh?"

"Your shoe." He pointed down at my feet.

I glanced down. Lo and behold, there was a strand of pumpkin guts on my right shoe, with a couple of pumpkin seeds dangling off the side.

"Oh that?" I replied with a nervous chuckle. "No, I wasn't smashing pumpkins."

"Well then how did that get on your shoe?"

"Well, I met up with Ben, Liz, and Sierra earlier. Some other kids had been smashing pumpkins. We helped clean it up and some must have fallen on my shoe," I replied, hoping he would take the bait, and quite proud of myself for thinking on the fly so quickly.

He gave me a side-eyed glance before finally shrugging it off.

"Well, hey! Good news! Your drawing got an award for the best Halloween art this year! Isn't that neat?"

"Yeah, the whole town was gushing over it." Mom hollered from the kitchen.

"Oh...that's so...cool!"

"Hey, didn't you order food?" she asked, as she entered the living room. "The $20 is still sitting there."

"Huh? What? No, I uh, just munched. I wasn't hungry earlier."

"Well, we can always order food now," Dad said. "I'm starving. All they had at the museum was fruit platters."

The three of us had a nice chuckle over that.

We ordered pizza and decided to play a quick board game before heading to bed. I wound up falling asleep with little effort after the long and difficult evening. I was exhausted.

The next few days at school flew by. Sierra, Kelly, and their boyfriends were much nicer to us now. None of us bothered to tell our parents what happened. Ben told his parents the scrape on his head came from him tripping and falling. Classic.

Regarding the Pumpkin Man? Everything in town calmed down. There were no new news reports, and everything went back to normal. The hustle and bustle of Halloween and trick or treat swept across the city once more.

Ben, Liz, Sierra, Kelly and I took the opportunity for a fresh start in friendship and ran with it. We didn't dare utter Johnny Rotten's name anymore.

By the time Friday evening rolled around, it was Halloween night. Time for trick or treat, and I couldn't have been more excited. We had a *huge* group going this year – Ben, Liz, Sierra, Kelly, Bryce, Tyler and me. Bryce and Ben had a heart to heart after hearing about the Johnny Rotten incidents. Bryce said he always acted tough in front of others but wasn't sure he would've stood up to a living nightmare the way Ben had. Ben had definitely grown more confident in himself since that day and all our parents had converged. They thought it was great seeing us go trick-or-treating together.

Everyone was meeting at my house.

That evening, I went into the bathroom to put my costume together and look at myself in the mirror. I was delighted with how my costume had turned out. I looked very spooky indeed.

I went downstairs and sat on the couch to wait.

Time passed, and the doorbell rang. I got up and answered it. Everyone was outside waiting for me. This was the largest group I had ever trick-or-treated with, and I was so excited.

We started our excursion in the neighborhood, collecting candy from the local community. Soon, we arrived at an old house with black siding, all the lights inside were off. The only light on was the porch light.

I approached and rang the doorbell.

The door slowly creaked open, revealing a darkness in the home, but no one standing there.

My heart raced. I wasn't sure what was going on.

"Trick or treat?" I asked.

"HAHAHAHA!" A deep monstrous laugh bellowed from within the home. My heart began beating like a drum.

"Happy Halloween!" The deep monstrous voice boomed. Suddenly, Johnny Rotten lunged forward and grabbed hold of me. "You are mine now and forever!"

I struggled to free myself from Johnny Rotten's grip. "No! Let me go!"

Suddenly, my whole body began shaking.

"Emily! Wake up! Emily!" My dad cried. I let out an ear-piercing shriek as he kept a hold of me.

"Honey...honey. You were having a nightmare," My dad said. I scanned the room and realized I'd fallen asleep while waiting for everyone.

I gave my dad a giant hug. "Oh, thank God it's you!"

"Of course, it's me! Who else would it be?" he asked returning my hug. "Now go on and have fun. All your friends are here."

A wave of relief passed over me. I grabbed my candy basket and headed out to meet everyone. They all had amazing costumes on.

I guess when it was all said and done, I got what I wished for. This was the most frightening Halloween yet.

We hurried down the driveway to begin our trick or treating journey. I took one last look back at Johnny Rotten.

I could have sworn I saw his head move.

A NOTE FROM THE AUTHOR

First of all, I wanted to say thank you all so much for continuing with the Scareville series. It means the world to me to have your support. My love for horror and ability to provide a fun, yet scary atmosphere for you all to enjoy, brings my heart such warmth.

I started on this journey not really sure what to expect, but the outpouring of support has really given me a new hope in life, and I hope that my love for this translates to all of you who are reading as well.

I want to stress that all of you should pursue your dreams. No matter how farfetched they seem. Passion, hard work, and enjoying what you do are the founding blocks to being successful in life. If others don't share your vision, that's okay. Prove them wrong and show them.

I love and value all of you out there reading this, as you have clearly taken an interest in my life and this series. I hope you will continue to follow along with me.

I'm just getting started.

Be sure to stay up to date with the Scareville series!

#1. Welcome to Scareville
#2. How to Create a Monster

And up next...the third book in the Scareville series! Be on the lookout for:

#3 Monsters of Mt. Hope

I WANT YOU FOR
SCAREVILLE
EST
20
25
ARMY
JOIN NOW!

THE END?

Not if you want to dive into more of Crystal Lake Publishing's Tales from the Darkest Depths!

For our mature horror books, check out our amazing website and online store or download our latest catalog here. https://geni.us/CLPCatalog

We always have great new projects and content on the website to dive into, as well as a newsletter, behind the scenes options, social media platforms, our own dark fiction shared-world series and our very own webstore. Our webstore even has categories specifically for KU books, non-fiction, anthologies, and of course more novels and novellas.

Readers...

Thank you for reading *How To Create a Monster*. We hope you enjoyed this entry into the Scareville Universe.

If you have a moment, please review *How To Create a Monster* at the store where you bought it.
Help other readers by telling them why you enjoyed this book. No need to write an in-depth discussion. Even a single sentence will be greatly appreciated. Reviews go a long way to helping a book sell, and is great for an author's career. It'll also help us to continue publishing quality books.

Thank you again for taking the time to journey with Crystal Lake Publishing.
You will find links to all our social media platforms on our Linktree page.
https://linktr.ee/CrystalLakePublishing

Follow us on Amazon:

MISSION STATEMENT

Since its founding in August 2012, Crystal Lake has quickly become one of the world's leading publishers of Dark Fiction and Horror books. In 2023, Crystal Lake officially transitioned into an entertainment company, joining several other divisions, genres, and imprints, including Torrid Waters, Crystal Lake Comics, Crystal Lake Games, Crystal Lake Kids, and many more.

While we strive to present only the highest quality fiction and entertainment, we also endeavour to support authors along their writing journey. We offer our time and experience in non-fiction projects, as well as author mentoring and services, at competitive prices.

With several Bram Stoker Award wins and many other wins and nominations (including the HWA's Specialty Press Award), Crystal Lake Publishing puts integrity, honor, and respect at the forefront of our publishing operations.

We strive for each book and outreach program we spearhead to not only entertain and touch or comment on issues that affect our readers, but also to strengthen and support the Dark Fiction field and its authors.

Not only do we find and publish authors we believe are destined for greatness, but we strive to work with men and women who endeavour to be decent human beings who care more for others than themselves, while still being hard working, driven, and passionate artists and storytellers.

Crystal Lake Publishing is and will always be a beacon of what passion and dedication, combined with overwhelming teamwork and respect, can accomplish. We endeavour to know each and every one of our readers, while building personal relationships with our authors, reviewers, bloggers, podcasters, bookstores, and libraries.

We will be as trustworthy, forthright, and transparent as any business can be, while also keeping most of the headaches away from our authors, since it's our job to solve the problems so they can stay in a creative mind. Which of course also means paying our authors.

We do not just publish books, we present to you worlds within your world, doors within your mind, from talented authors who sacrifice so much for a moment of your time.

There are some amazing small presses out there, and through collaboration and open forums we will continue to support other presses in the goal of helping authors and showing the world what quality small presses are capable of accomplishing. No one wins when a small press goes down, so we will always be there to support hardworking, legitimate presses and their authors. We don't see Crystal Lake as the best press out there, but we will always strive to be the best, strive to be the most interactive and grateful, and even blessed press around. No matter what happens over time, we will also take our mission very seriously while appreciating where we are and enjoying the journey.

What do we offer our authors that they can't do for themselves through self-publishing?

We are big supporters of self-publishing (especially hybrid publishing), if done with care, patience, and planning. However, not every author has the time or inclination to do market research, advertise, and set up book launch strategies. Although a lot of authors are successful in doing it all, strong small presses will always be there for the authors who just want to do what they do best: write.

What we offer is experience, industry knowledge, contacts and trust built up over years. And due to our strong brand and trusting fanbase, every Crystal Lake Publishing book comes with weight of respect. In time our fans begin to trust our judgment and will try a new author purely based on our support of said author.

With each launch we strive to fine-tune our approach, learn from our mistakes, and increase our reach. We continue to assure our authors that we're here for them and that we'll carry the weight of the launch and dealing with third parties while they focus on their strengths—be it writing, interviews, blogs, signings, etc.

We also offer several mentoring packages to authors that include knowledge and skills they can use in both traditional and self-publishing endeavours.

We look forward to launching many new careers.

This is what we believe in. What we stand for. This will be our legacy.

Welcome to Crystal Lake Publishing—Where Stories Come Alive!

www.ingramcontent.com/pod-product-compliance
Lightning Source LLC
Chambersburg PA
CBHW031052310726
48969CB00007B/2242